TRUE NORTH

TRUE NORTH

A NOVEL OF THE UNDERGROUND RAILROAD

KATHRYN LASKY

Scholastic Inc.
New York Toronto London Auckland Sydney
Mexico City New Delhi Hong Kong Buenos Aires

No part of this publication may be reproduced, stored in a
retrieval system, or transmitted in any form or by any means,
electronic, mechanical, photocopying, recording, or otherwise,
without written permission of the publisher. For information
regarding permission, please write to: Permissions Department,
Scholastic Inc., 557 Broadway, New York, New York 10012.

This book was originally published in hardcover by the Blue Sky Press in 1996.

ISBN–13: 978-0-545-08802-2
ISBN–10: 0-545-08802-X

Special thanks to Joan Giurdanella for her careful fact checking.
The Plantation Era colloquial speech in this book was adapted from several sources,
including oral histories in *Bullwhip Days: The Slaves Remember*, edited by James Mello

12 11 10 9 8 7 6 5 4 3 2 1   9 10 11 12 13 14/0

Printed in the U.S.A.   40
This edition first printing, January 2009

TRUE NORTH

Prologue

Diary entry of Lucy Bradford Wentworth

1917

154 Beacon Street,
Boston, Massachusetts

I'm trying to remember now exactly how it happened. It's like trying to recall the precise steps of a very complicated dance after all these years. But, in fact, I do remember.

I had waited until after the wedding ceremony, hidden in a closet beyond the vestry of King's Chapel. I had a clear view of everyone. Mama looked very solemn, but radiant in her moss-green watered silk. On her head she wore a small satin bonnet with snowy explosions of egret plumes. My sisters, the bridesmaids, moved like a procession of cabbage roses, their large pink faces framed by cascades of golden curls. And finally Iris, the bride — in a cloud of orange blossoms, her dress not quite white, but with a hint of the palest blue, like the blue that flushes the milky throat of her namesake flower.

Yet at the sight of my father's face, I gasped. I had been away for months, and in that time he had become an old man.

When the ceremony finally ended, I slipped out the back of the church with my coat wrapped tightly around me, and from Temple Place I watched the broughams, family landaus, and coupés take the guests to the reception. The bridal couple was, of course, the first to leave in Grandfather's old coupé, the one kept in Brookline. Its leather gleamed, the brass fittings bright under the wintry sky.

I followed on foot back to our house at 136 Beacon Street. It wasn't far, not after the distances I had traveled. I sneaked in the back, through the walled kitchen garden, and into the coal keep. The fires had been going for hours, and this would probably be a safe place. I had forgotten that the entrance to the wine cellar led off the same hallway.

How was I supposed to know that it was an old family custom, obviously not from the Boston side, for the parents of the bride to come forth with some ridiculous heirloom bottle of champagne for the final toast to the newlywed couple? And according to custom, they were both supposed to carry it from the musty old cellar where it had rested since their own wedding, when it had been brought up from the Virginia plantation of my mother.

I must have been dozing before nature's call became so sharp, for surely I would have heard my parents talking as they went to the wine cellar. But I had heard nothing. Thinking that the coast was clear, I chose to step out from my hiding place at the precise moment my parents emerged from the cellar.

My mother shrieked and fainted. My father turned pale and then began crying. There was a great commotion as people came rushing into the small hallway. Cook, I think, fainted, and little Mary, the scullery girl, squealed as if she had just been impaled by one of the carving knives she was charged with keeping sharp. "It's Lucy! She's dead! But here is her ghost!" she screamed.

I don't really remember much after that.

For a long time I believed that all my sisters

blamed me for spoiling the wedding. After all, until that moment, they had thought for months that I was dead, had drowned. I think, however, they were actually happy to see me alive and well, even if my timing, as usual, was inopportune.

Has it truly been fifty-nine years since I last saw Afrika? I cannot believe it. It seems like yesterday.

Chapter 1
January 1858
Great Dismal Swamp, Virginia

Afrika stared up the gleaming barrel of the flintlock pistol that pointed directly down at her head. It looked old, all right, but oiled and cleaned; she could almost smell the wadding and the powder. And she didn't doubt for one second that Miss Harriet would use it.

"You go on with me or you die," the woman rasped. The scar creasing her forehead looked slick in the moonlight.

This would be a darned good time for Miss Harriet to have one of her famous sleeping spells. Afrika had yet to see one, though they had been traveling together for almost a week. The others had talked about them. How Miss Harriet could be standing up straight and singing one of her

1

songs and suddenly fall asleep right in the middle of it. Why couldn't she do that now?

"Look here. I ain't going back." Afrika tried to keep her voice firm. She knew that Miss Harriet Tubman didn't tolerate whiners. Miss Harriet had gone far out of her way on this trip — all the way down to southern Virginia. And although there were handbills offering big rewards for her capture — up to $40,000 — plastered all over Maryland, Delaware, and Virginia, Harriet Tubman usually stuck to eastern Maryland, to Dorchester County.

Afrika looked down at the little bit of a thing pulsating in her hands, a baby too small to even cradle in her arms. Would slip right through the crook of her elbow.

"That baby going to die!" Harriet barked.

A steely edge as hard as the barrel of that flintlock crept into Afrika's voice. "Yeah. And I'm going to be with her when her spirit flies off. I'm going to give her a good sending, then I'm going to run."

Harriet Tubman knew when she'd been licked. Knew when it wasn't any use to continue a standoff. This girl with flint in her voice and dead eyes wasn't going to turn around and go back. No slave catcher would force anything out of her. She lowered the pistol.

"All right, when that baby dies, you wrap it up and put it over there by that cypress stump. Then you find that oily hole and slather yourself good. No slave-catching dog will be able to follow you with that muck on you. Covers any human scent. You strike straight out across from that hole, and you go at a good clip. Soon you see the swamp be getting marshy. At the edge of the marsh, there's a shed. If you see an old chicken coop with its gate open, you know it's safe to go in there, and someone will be by for you."

Then she was gone.

Afrika looked down at that life in her hands, that life that had slipped out of her a half hour before. Wasn't supposed to come for another three months or more. And she couldn't believe it when she saw it.

It was a little girl, and she glistened in Afrika's palms like an ebony moon. And to think how Afrika had spent all that time hating the unborn child. She knew she was in trouble the first time he laid eyes on her. She'd nightmared all these months about some little pale, red-haired baby popping out. But, no, this weren't no carrot. It was her little moon, her own little baby girl moon.

It was her warm hands, Miss Harriet said, that made the baby live the extra minutes. Afrika had hoped that the baby might open her eyes. A quick hello good-bye. Afrika wanted the baby to know that her mama thought she was beautiful and warn't no carrot baby. But when she put her lips against the baby's black skin and felt for a quiver, there was none. She didn't cry. Not one tear. No regrets. Maybe it was better that the baby didn't open her eyes and see her.

She worked quickly now. And she didn't do what Miss Harriet told her. Miss Harriet wanted her to use her baby to decoy the hounds. She'd decoy them all right, but she wasn't having her baby eaten by any slave-hunting dogs. She'd escaped, and she'd make sure her baby did, too.

Afrika took the baby down to the oily hole. Still holding the baby in her palms, she dunked her own arms up to the elbows. Then she grabbed some broad skunk cabbage leaves and wrapped her moon baby up like a bun. Where to put her?

Just ahead she spotted a black gum tree. A

crack of moonlight revealed a narrow hollow high up. That's where she'd put her baby girl. Too high for the hounds, and they'd never smell her anyway with the oil. Owl might find her, feed her to the young ones. That was all right. She had no complaint with owls.

Afrika stuck her package down the front of her dress and clawed up the tree, just six or seven feet, no more, to the first branch. She swung herself up onto it. Then, standing on the branch, she reached for the hollow. She took out her package — it had gotten a little mashed — and shoved it in the hollow. Then she swung down under the branch and dropped lightly to the ground.

It was at that moment that she heard them, a creaking sound like wind in the trees. But it wasn't wind. Miss Harriet had warned her that this was how the dogs sounded when you first heard them — like the creak of an old tree leaning into the wind. But these dogs weren't going to get her baby, her own little baby girl moon. She was free.

Afrika didn't wait for the next creak. She took off for the oily hole and scooped up handfuls of sludge and slathered it over her until she was as black as her moon baby. But she couldn't think about that baby anymore and the death that might be waiting for her. She had to think about dogs and cottonmouths. She had to run through that swamp and be smart. Most important, she had to think about the freedom coming. Dying was easy — being alive was the hard part.

As she moved out into the water beyond the oily hole, she heard the hounds clearly. She could even hear the men's boots stomping and breaking through the brush. Between these sounds, however, her ear caught something else. It swelled in the night. And then, like a long velvet ribbon unfurling in the darkness of the swamp, there was the soft *whooo whooo* of an owl.

Chapter 2

January 1858

Boston, Massachusetts

Lucy Bradford sat on the steep steps that led up to her house at 136 Beacon Street and squinted into the fog that rolled in from the sea. It was so thick, she could hardly see the house across the street, and the iron tips of the fence not five feet from her floated like lost punctuation marks in the yellow clouds.

The day was unusually warm for the time of year, and something in the drafts of mist reminded her of hurricane weather. Unfortunately, in Lucy's lifetime one had never hit Boston. Oh, they would come close, but then somehow they would veer off just before Boston.

Now with her grandfather, it was another story. He had not only met hurricanes right here in Boston, he had sailed out to greet them! Levi

Bradford had worked in the China trade on Bradford family ships before he had settled down to doctoring.

Lucy wrinkled her nose and sniffed harder. Gracious! What she wouldn't give right now for just a plain old hurricane — not a nor'easter, they didn't count. Nor'easters were as common as mud. No, she wanted a storm that came in like a pack of scalded cats on tropical air. She wanted winds that blistered the varnish off wood and split it to smithereens.

Lucy Bradford was not destructive. She was bored. And as she sat on her front doorstep, she wondered if it was possible to die of boredom.

She certainly knew the cause of it — her oldest sister Iris's wedding. The engagement had been announced at New Year's, but the wedding itself was still several months off. She had been excited when her parents had made the announcement of their firstborn's engagement to Mr. Elwyn Van Schuyler of New York City. "Quite the catch!" pronounced Aunt Ruby, never one to mince words, in tones slightly less audible than a fog signal, causing Lucy's mother to tinge pink.

Within a few days, the excitement had worn off for Lucy, and she merely wanted to get on with life as usual. What she had failed to realize was that life would never be usual again, at least not until Iris and Elwyn were "hitched," as Pap put it.

Originally Elwyn had hoped for an earlier wedding, something in late summer. No! No no no no no no! A chorus of no's virtually rained down on the poor fellow's head from Emeralda, Lucy's mother, and all the aunts — Ruby, Pearl, and Opal, not to mention the bride and all her sisters — Rose, Daisy, and Delphinia.

But not from Lucy, who was the youngest. Lucy thought that April was a lovely time to get married. The magnolias would be in bloom, the heat would be bearable, the marshy area of the Back Bay wouldn't be smelly yet. But these were not considered relevant issues by the bride, her mother, her aunts, and her sisters. How would they ever be able to find a house in New York by then and fit it out? And the Dozens — how in heaven's name could they ever get the Dozens done any sooner?

The Dozens were the curses of Lucy's life. They were a cruel custom that yoked every female relative and every female servant in the bridal household to an embroidery hoop. For hours on end, the women embroidered what would be the bride's initials once she had a new name. As much as Lucy liked Elwyn, she could just kill him for having that fancy double-barreled New York name — Van Schuyler!! Instead of three stupid letters, she had to embroider four: **I VS B**.

Lucy's mother had made her a little template so she could trace the design onto each tea towel and handkerchief she was expected to embroider. There had to be several dozen of each. When Lucy had complained, her mother was shocked. "It truly is an honor, dear. You are fourteen years old now. A young lady. And we so want you to feel included."

Lucy didn't believe it for one moment. Did Mary, the scullery girl, and Bridget, the upstairs maid, and Mrs. Hudson, the laundress, think it was such an honor? "Well, it's part of their job," her mother explained. "They get paid," Lucy countered. "Well, yes, that's true." A perplexed look had crossed Emeralda Bradford's fine-boned face. "Could I get paid?" Lucy had asked.

"What?" It was more of a gasp than a word.

Emeralda's hand plunged into the deep folds of her dress and drew out the little vial of smelling salts.

"Lucy, the wedding will be fun. I guarantee that. It will be fun!" her father had said earnestly — too earnestly. "Your mother and I are quite concerned about this money talk."

"Money talk?"

Her father coughed and lowered his chin as he did when uncomfortable with a subject. Her mother, however, plunged right in with a forthrightness worthy of Aunt Ruby. "It's coarse, dear, to talk about money. Let alone ask if you can be paid."

"Coarse . . . money?"

"Yes, darling." Her father was more comfortable now. "It just isn't done in polite society — talk about money."

"But I don't understand." Lucy had been genuinely perplexed. It had seemed to her that money was all that polite society, particularly her family, ever talked about. How much the woolen mills in the Thayer branch of the family were making, and what with some new regulations they might be obliged to increase the mill girls' wages, and, of course, how Elwyn Van Schuyler himself was considered a catch because he had money and was not one of those idle fortune hunters with only a good name.

Lucy thought about this as she sat on the steps. All the family ever did talk about was money! In many ways her family was as dense as the fog that swirled about her now.

Just then she heard voices melting out of the mist. Good Lord! It was her sisters, back already from one of the innumerable luncheons honoring Iris. She was supposed to have had the stupid fingertip towel embroidered, and she hadn't finished one blasted letter. Oh, she didn't want to face them now.

The fog, of course! The perfect camouflage. Why couldn't she just skip down two blocks to Pap's at 154? She'd stay up late tonight and embroider an extra tea towel to make up for it, and maybe even a handkerchief.

Lucy stood up. The mist had grown denser. The iron fence tips were just dull smudges. She felt for the fence to guide her down the last step. The gaslights hung like dim, lusterless pearls on the fog-thick street. She inhaled the smell of cod and kelp that blew in from the sea.

A phantom in a top hat whispered by her. She heard the click of his cane on the brick sidewalk. Ahead there was the creak of a carriage and the clop of the hooves of a matched pair. With the toe of her high-button shoe, she felt for the curb. She drew her pelisse more tightly around her. A silly garment to wear out in a fog. The thick, nubbly knit drew beads of moisture until it fairly shimmered. Seed pearls, she thought. Oh dear! Seed pearls — wedding dresses. Would this wedding invade everything?

Chapter 3

January 1858

Northeast Edge of the Great Dismal Swamp,

Virginia

T*hat ain't going to fit this pickaninny. Just
going to chew up her leg, and she won't be
worth the salt to season your food by time we get
her to Richmond. Just tie her with that hank of rope
there."*

*Afrika didn't know what was happening. Why was
this man fussing so with her ankles? And where
was Mama? Then she felt herself being lifted up
onto the wagon. It wasn't a bad feeling. Kind of
like flying. She'd just stick out her arms and see
what happened. . . . There, she saw it, little fluffs
sprouting out, downy, just like puffs on nestlings.
"My goodness, my feathers growing fast," she said
to a little boy who was crying the wettest tears she'd
ever seen. "You want to grow some, too? I got my*

beautiful flying feathers." Indeed her arms were swept now with strong layers of beautiful tawny feathers, black ones and brown ones, a few reddish ones. But Wet Tears looked at her dumbly. "I'm going to try out these here wings. Fly over Mama and Old Cud. Wave bye-bye to that snarly, ugly-faced baby up at the great house who makes my mama's day one long misery. She says I'm such a good child; now I'm going to be a bird child."

Afrika giggled, and then she started to spread her wings. Just as she was about to lift up, just as a draft of sweet air caught like the softest pillow under her wing arms, a hot scalding scream tore apart the very air. She saw her mama's face, twisted and terrible. "Not my baby!"

Overseer stepped up. "Master done sold your Frieda!"

Her mama clawed at his face. He raised his stick, and the sweet face split open and poured blood. Afrika's wings folded up. The feathers were falling off her arms and drifting in lazy, maddening little swirls toward the pools of blood gushing from her mama's face. Then the feathers, the brown ones, the black ones, the red ones, all the lovely feathers began to squirm before her eyes. They became fat green tobacco worms. They were crawling out of her mother's face. Great streams of them. "Where are my feathers? Where are my feathers? Mama! Mama!"

Afrika's eyes flew open. She clapped her hand over her mouth, biting her palm. Had she really screamed out "Mama" from her dream? What if someone had heard her? She froze, too scared to breathe. How could she have done that after waiting all those endless hours in the cold, drizzling rain for the signal that it was safe for her to enter the shed?

When she had arrived at the edge of the marsh, she spied the shack from the tall grass, but it had been too dark to see if the chicken coop's gate was open. She didn't dare risk creeping out from her hiding place. It had been the right decision because at the first thin light of the dawn, she saw that the gate was shut.

Huddled in the grass, she waited. It became colder and colder with each hour. She watched as a thin coat of ice formed on the mud. Squatting on her heels, she watched the sky fade to a dusky gray. The drizzle began. She tried not to sleep, but every once in a while she would nod off, then jerk awake, causing the marsh grass to tremble and possibly betray her. Finally she gave up and settled into the mud, curling herself tight as a snail. In this manner she had slept fitfully for short stretches at a time.

Every now and then, upon waking, she would raise her head to see if the coop's gate was open. But it was not until late in the afternoon that she was awakened by a creak. Through the marsh grass, she saw the coop. Its gate was wide open. A bent figure scurried off into the deepening shadows.

Inside the shack she found, wrapped in fresh white muslin, an ash cake and a few pieces of dried herring, which she ate hungrily. Then she had straight away fallen asleep. But it hadn't felt like sleep. The images of the terrible dream still seared her brain. Well, at least her little baby would never have a dream like that.

Afrika knew how to count. She learned from picking worms off tobacco plants, or maybe earlier, down at Talleystone on the rows of cotton she had worked. She wondered how many beats that baby heart had made — as many as the rows of cotton she picked in a week? As many as the worms on a dozen plants in a bad time? As many seeds as in a cucumber? She had been thinking about this for a spell when she heard footsteps outside.

"Friend?" The voice was low and hoarse.

Chapter 4

January 1858

Boston, Massachusetts

Lucy had arrived at the immense carved door of number 154 Beacon. She pulled the doorbell hard. Within a minute, no more, the great brass knob turned, and the door swung open.

"Your pap's not in, Miss Lucy. But you come on. He should be back directly." Zephy's face glowed like a polished horse chestnut in the thick fog. Lucy always thought that if she were to be another color, she would like to be the color of Zephy.

Now she stepped into the hush and solemn shadows of her grandfather's house. The gas jet was turned down low. She first glanced at the cane stand. The hickory one with the ivory head was missing. This confirmed Pap's absence. Sometimes Zephy told callers that Doctor was out when he really wasn't. Once Zephy had started to tell her that Pap was out, but when she saw Lucy's eyes dart to the cane stand, she said, "Just a minute." Zephy had then led Lucy into the kitchen to have a mug of cider until her grandfather could see her.

Dr. Levi Bradford had always been considered a bit of an odd duck. Somewhat reclusive, he eschewed the more traditional gathering spots of proper Bostonians. Since his beloved wife, Maribel, had died, he had become decidedly less inclined to do the things expected of a man of his prominence and social standing. Since Maribel's death, he, at a point when most men would be winding down their careers, seemed to have stepped up his own. He continued to see all of his old patients and had added a new lecture series this year to his teaching at the Harvard Medical College. It also seemed that he was endlessly attending meetings of some sort or another.

Lucy followed Zephy through the dim light of the entry hall, past the monumental walnut sideboard. Zephy opened the double doors to the library.

"Want me to bring you something to eat, Miss Lucy?"

"No. I'm fine. Thank you, Zephy."

Zephy retreated and closed the doors as she left.

Lucy glanced quickly at the huge grandfather clock to see if by some strange miracle it was working. It was not. Its hands were still fixed at two o'clock. They had been fixed at two o'clock ever since Lucy could remember. Called a leviathan because of its immense size, the clock rose a full eight feet from its base to the top of its pediment.

Built of mahogany, the clock seemed to grow like a tree against the east wall of the library. It had been given to Maribel and Levi Bradford as a wedding present and had worked for the first five minutes of a marriage that lasted another fifty years. It was handsome, however, and Levi had grown quite attached to it.

Her grandfather's library was just about Lucy's favorite place to be in the whole world. It seemed to be a kind of universe unto itself, with its odd curios and shelf upon shelf of leather-bound books. Human skulls used for anatomy lessons, side by side with numerous bird skeletons, graced inlaid tables. Her grandfather had a passion for birds, especially raptors. Of late, he had taken quite a fancy to owls and had begun going out in the evenings to his estate in Brookline on what he called owling expeditions.

On another table was a model of the sleek sloop *Winsome*, aboard which he often took Lucy for a sail through Boston Harbor and out to the harbor islands. He had taught her how to hold a steady course and had even begun to explain the rudiments of compass and celestial navigation. All over the library were Indian artifacts brought back by cousin Francis Parkman on his trips west.

For Lucy there was a ritual upon entering the room. After glancing at the clock, she would go to the coat tree in the corner and take down the fringed buckskin jacket. Slipping into it, she would next give her arms a little shake just to hear the soft whisper of the fringe. In the bottom drawer of a tea caddy brought back on one of the Bradford China trade ships, there was not tea at all but a handsome pair of beaded Sioux moccasins. After unbuttoning her shoes, she would slip into the moccasins. Then she would select a book, or perhaps a bone or a bird skeleton to study or draw, and repair to Pap's big walnut desk. If Pap were there, she would still sit at the desk, and he would sit in his chair by the fire where he could simultaneously watch her as well as the fire.

Right now she climbed up the library ladder and fetched the anatomy book. Her colored pencils were where she had left them, in the top drawer of the walnut desk. She had finished off the esophagus the previous day. Now she was halfway through the pyloric sphincter, which she had chosen to draw in an elegant purple color.

So absorbed was she in her drawing that she did not hear the familiar tattoo of the hickory cane in the foyer. The doors swung open.

"What'll it be, guts or Gaul?"

"Pap!"

An immense man, well over six feet tall, with unruly white hair swirling about his head like a minor tornado, filled the door frame. His face was gaunt, his nose a jutting blade, his eyes deep set and the color of blue smoke. He wore a black cutaway coat, an amber-colored silk vest, a black silk cravat, and dark trousers.

He strode over to the desk. "Ah, guts it is! The venerable pyloric sphincter works just like the drawstrings on a purse, unless it's been chewed up by excessive consumption of spirits. Speaking of which — Zephyra, might you fetch me a pot of tea with a splash of brandy in it — dispels the effects of the fog."

"Yes, sir," answered Zephy, who was standing in the doorway still holding Pap's tall hat and mackintosh.

Five minutes later, Levi Bradford had slipped into a well-worn black silk jacket embroidered with a herd of scarlet dragons. On his head he wore a quilted, tasseled cap, and on his feet were a pair of Indian moccasins.

"Grocer's boy just came over. He says a shipment of them special dates will be coming through, Doctor."

Levi Bradford looked up. "Ah, the ones from the Levant?" A sudden spark was fanned in the blue smoke of his eyes.

"Yes, grocer says they'll be coming in the next week — if you want him to reserve a package for you."

"By all means, by all means. Thank you, Zephy. Thank you."

Levi Bradford cleared his throat noisily and poured himself a cup of tea. "So how do the wedding plans go?"

There was a low growl from Lucy.

"Now how am I to interpret that?"

Lucy put down her colored pencil and looked straight at her grandfather. "Exceedingly well and decidedly boring."

Levi Bradford suppressed a chuckle. There was no one quite like Lucy. He had never encountered anyone whose physiognomy and spirit were so perfectly aligned. Her curly blue-black hair framed the heart-shaped pale face that could never be called delicate because it drew into a tough little chin. And then there were her eyes. Across a room they appeared black, but closer up one began to realize they were not black at all but a deep midnight blue. Beneath her left eye, not much bigger than the head of a pin, was a dark freckle that lent a curious accent to all her expressions.

"I might, Pap, just die of boredom — total, complete boredom — rather like heart shock, I bet. Is it possible for the same thing to happen in the brain?"

"Possibly, possibly. Might make an interesting topic for luncheon tomorrow. I shall be going over to Cambridge. Iris and Elwyn still set on the October wedding date?"

"Yes. I think so. It all has to do with the wedding trip. Something about getting to Biarritz by spring and then Venice in July."

"Venice in July!" barked Levi. "Surely you must be mistaken. They want to expose their lungs, their entire respiratory system, to the evils of that cesspool in the heat of the summer? Promise me, dear child, that you will never go to Venice in the summer, not for a wedding trip or anything else."

"Of course not, Pap. I shall stay right here for my wedding trip."

"Well, you could go to Dover, or up to Beverly. Nantucket is quite lovely in the summer."

"No, Pap. I mean on this continent. I think I would like to go where cousin Francis Parkman goes — west — the Oregon Trail."

"Ah, Lucy!" Levi Bradford threw back his head and laughed. "Want to go sleep in a tepee and eat dog meat, do you? What will your parents think of that?"

"Cousin Francis said it was quite delicious when he had it with the Sioux." Lucy had read Francis Parkman's book twice already since its publication. And west was where she wanted to go. She wanted to see everything her cousin had seen — the rattlesnakes thick as a man's arm, the herds of elk with antlers clattering. She wanted to see a buffalo hunt. "But don't fret, Pap, my wedding trip is a long way off."

"I should hope so," Levi Bradford said emphatically.

"So before that, why don't you take me on an owling expedition . . . please, Pap! Please!"

"That reminds me, dear child. Francis came to see me yesterday at my office." He always changed the subject when she brought up owling. It was maddening. He had said he would take her sometime, but there never seemed to be a right time as far as Lucy could see.

"Oh dear, is he sick again?"

"I'm afraid his condition is a chronic one. Yes, his eyes are worse, and he must now dictate everything to a secretary over at Harvard. In any case he presented me with . . ." Levi Bradford gŏt up and went to a deep cabinet and opened it. "I have it here someplace. . . . Ah, here it is." With a flourish, he took out a very broad-brimmed hat. "Genuine article — a buffalo hunter's hat. Looks like it was chewed by a herd of mice and a bit fragrant at that. I had Zephy put it in a bag with some camphor flakes. Improved it some. Here, why don't you try it on?"

Lucy put it on. It slid halfway down her face, but she liked the feel of it. Tilting her head back so she could see out from under the brim, she spoke to her grandfather.

"Don't worry, Pap, about what Mama and Papa think of my wedding trip. By the time I get married, they'll be so worn out from giving weddings for Rose, Daisy, and Delphy that they'll just wave me off and not care where I go on my wedding trip. No horrible Dozens to embroider, no silly luncheons."

"Oh, now, Lucy!" Levi sighed.

"Don't feel sorry for me. It will be wonderful. Having five daughters is very tiring, Pap."

"Not to mention expensive."

"Yes. They'll probably run out of money by then, giving all these fancy weddings."

Old Levi grunted — as he always did when money was mentioned in terms of spending rather than investing.

"They'll run out of money just like they ran out of names," Lucy continued.

"Now what in heaven's name do you mean by that?"

Lucy tilted the hat back farther. "Well, Pap, you know as well as I do that by the time I came along, being the fifth girl and all, Mama and Papa had run out of flower names."

Levi Bradford stood up from his chair. "Lucy!" Pap's voice boomed. "You were not named Lucy because they ran out of flowers. Lord knows there are enough flowers to name the inhabitants of a small city. There is violet, and petunia, and lily, larkspur, dahlia, myrtle, ivy, zinnia."

"Myrtle!" The little dark freckle punctuated Lucy's horror. "How revolting!"

"Precisely," he continued. "Those were your grandmother's sentiments. She couldn't bear the thought of one more baby named for a flower.

'Pick a decent name,' she said. 'Or if you must name her for something, name her for a good person.' And then I said, how about a good ship?"

"A ship. That's a nice idea." Lucy brightened.

"Well, that is exactly what you were named for, child — a ship in the Bradford line."

"A ship named Lucy?"

"Not quite. There had always been a series of our China trade ships with the word 'light' in their name — starting with *Light Horse* back in the late 1700s out of Salem, then going on to *Light of Canton, Light of the Seas, North Light, Polar Light.* They had all done exceedingly well. *Light of Canton* survived the famous typhoon off Manila. Well, the name Light didn't have quite the right ring. So your grandmother suggested the name Lucy to your mother. This was the closest we could come — Lucy — deriving from the Latin word *lux* meaning light or lucent, shining."

"And Mama thought it was all right?"

"Well, it took her a little time to get used to it. You know your mother, being a Southerner and all. She has these notions, well, family traditions, and it was a very strong family tradition to name all these girls that seem to be born into her line — hardly any males — in terms of classes of things. Hence all the flower names for your sisters. Your mother and her sisters were named after precious gems and stones. But, yes, she agreed to name you Lucy and even admitted to me quite recently that she thinks it was a good idea — you being so different from your sisters." He paused. "And it's an apt name. For you handled *Winsome* quite sportily in that blow last fall. By Jove! I was bragging to Bearse about it. Tacked her right up there, you did, between those two barks under just a smidgen of sail — worthy of your great grandfather, Captain Horace Bradford. You've got a nice light touch on the wheel, and that reminds me, now that you've got sun sights mastered, we'll begin working on star sights. A bit trickier. Vega — Vega's always a good bet, especially this time of year. . . ."

"Lucy!" She whispered the name softly. So it wasn't because they had run out of flowers at all. She had been named for ships, ships that had survived gales, hurricanes. Ships that had carried teas

and silks and chinaware and nankeen across the seas. "Lucy!" She whispered the name again. Now for the first time she loved her name. Its meaning glimmered like a little star in her mind's eye, its sound suddenly like a chime in the night — "Lucy!"

Chapter 5

February 1858

South of Portsmouth, Virginia

There was a lot to think about. First, the clothes. They felt peculiar. She'd never before worn men's trousers; and although Afrika might be walking to freedom, her legs had never felt more bound up even though the trousers were big. It was like having boxes 'round her legs.

She had to learn how to walk, and it better be like a boy because when the raggedy colored man who whispered "friend" to her in the night came, he quick told her that she'd better walk like a boy and keep that hat pulled down and square those shoulders under that jacket. And what else? Afrika thought hard. How did men walk? They walked with their arms loose, but so did women. But maybe not quite as loose, and maybe they hunched their shoulders a little bit forward —

that was it! Men walked with their shoulders more in the lead, and women? They sort of slid their hips forward when they walked.

She'd get it. A tune suddenly popped into her head. It was from a game the children used to play in the quarters called "Pat the Juba," and it had just the right rhythm for hunching your shoulders forward and punching ahead like a man walking down the road.

> *Juba this and Juba that,*
> *Juba killed a yeller cat.*
> *Juba this and Juba that,*
> *Hold your partner where you at.*

But it be time for me to get off this road, Afrika thought. She remembered what the old man had told her. The countryside was thick with slave catchers and their Negro-hunting dogs. He told her that there were handbills made up already advertising the escaped slaves. There had been five in the group with Miss Harriet, and they described each one, including Afrika, right down to the space between her two front teeth. That was why the first thing the old man did was give her a piece of bone to shove into the space. She had to remember to take it out when she ate or she might lose it. There was so much to remember.

Afrika stayed in the woods for cover but had to make sure she was still following the main road. She would come out from the trees occasionally to check her direction. The North Star, the one everyone talked about that pointed the way to freedom, had disappeared nights ago. Since she'd been in the swamp, there had not been a clear sky. But Miss Harriet had told them all about the moss growing on the north side of the trees. "They be like a whole chain of little stars on earth," Miss Harriet had said. And in this woods off the road to Little Chuckatuck Creek, the moss grew thick and spongy, and it became the sweetest touch in the world. Afrika had thought she couldn't feel anything with her hands anymore, they were so calloused from the tobacco, but it was as if on these starless nights feeling crept back into them, and it started right with the fingertips. It was as if freedom's way was so powerful, it poked right through the thick, hard skin.

She was heading for Little Chuckatuck Creek, and then as soon as she had crossed the creek, there was supposed to be a hill with a cemetery, and she was to hide there until the next friend came along. The distance from where she had started, from the shed to Little Chuckatuck Creek, was not far — maybe fifteen miles. But with dipping into the woods and all, it would stretch to twenty or twenty-five — two nights of walking. The old man had told her to be sure not to cross the creek too far south where it was deep and dangerous and the currents were swift.

She'd been traveling in the woods for almost three hours and still had not found the creek. Bone tired, she decided to take herself a little nap, because when she did find it, there would still be another mile to walk upstream, and she wanted to be fresh in order to cross. *Just a little nap,* she thought. Then, straight ahead, as if inviting her to come rest, was a hollowed-out place in the spreading roots of a black gum tree. Settling in, she curled herself up. The trousers were warmer than her dress. Soon she was asleep.

It was never clear to Afrika whether she had been sleeping or dreaming when she first felt it. But it seeped into her like a fine night mist, this fear, this dread. And then it was as if the inside of her eyelids were suddenly streaked with light.

This don't make sense, Afrika thought. No moon, no stars. She opened her eyes slowly. Patrollers! A cold fear seized her. Not thirty yards away, arcs of light swept through the bare, black trees. She heard a night bird screech and then the long, sputtering blow from a horse's nostrils. Suddenly the woods danced with shadows of men and horses. The thud of hooves mixed with the baying of dogs.

She didn't even think. One minute she was down, the next she was up and running. She didn't know which way. She just ran, immense, long strides gobbling up the ground, but the hounds were behind her. She heard a *whoop* from a man as his horse lunged through the trees. A limb reached out and swept off her hat. Suddenly the sky cleared off, and silver poured through the branches, flooding the woods. It was as if a torrent of light had been unleashed from above. The crack of a rifle split the night, hitting a tree branch in front of her.

She shouldn't be running straight. Too good a target, running straight. She needed to zigzag. She swung left. Surely the creek would come up soon. She had to get to that creek with running water.

They wouldn't be able to track her. The dogs couldn't track through water. She'd been a fool for falling asleep. Fool! Fool! No time to scold. She zagged again. Suddenly the ground dropped off. She heard a rustling, tumbling sound — *water!*

Scrambling down the bank, she gasped as she saw the creek, frothy and turbulent in the moonlight. The old man had said it would be still and shallow where she crossed. She leaned up against a tree. Something spongy and soft touched her palm. Moss. Moss on this side. Lordy! She'd been running the wrong way. She'd been running south.

Then the terrible baying began again, pouring out of the night like blood. She could feel their teeth. She knew about these dogs. They loved blood. That overseer, he was good with the dogs. Those slave-catchers knew how to feed the dogs to make them mean. They taught them the taste of blood, so that was all the dogs craved. Afrika had heard tell that a starving, slave-catching dog would eat its own pup if it were really hungry.

She looked at the water. Her knees began to tremble. She'd drown. But maybe that would be better than being torn up by dogs. Old Henry at Marlymont, he had half his face chewed off by a dog. One eye gone. Just half a nose with one hole to breathe out of. Little rag of an ear. Miss Harriet said when she left that she had a right to two things — her freedom and her death. Afrika guessed she might not get one, and the dogs wouldn't have the other.

Afrika pushed forward. Churning water swirled around her. The water was up to her thighs, then to her waist, but she kept walking. It ran fast, but she kept her footing. The water still rose. She didn't know what she would do if it came above her head. She didn't know how to swim.

Soon it was above her chest, her shoulders, and then a collar of white foam lapped at her neck. The current pulled her, too. It became harder to keep her feet on the bottom. But for some strange reason she was no longer frightened. She had made her decision, and the decision was that the dogs wouldn't get her.

And soon it seemed as if she was rising, being lifted from the creek. The water was down to her collarbone, and then to her chest, and then to her waist. She felt the ground firmly underfoot. But the current was still pulling. And suddenly a vision seemed to explode in her brain.

She looked up, and sure enough, there it was, twinkling fiercely in the indigo sky, scraped clear now of clouds — the North Star! And the current was pulling her to it. Lifted by invisible wings and pulled by the current, she headed north. So although she had never before swum, she had the unmistakable feeling that she might be able to float, and if she could float she could ride this current.

Slowly she picked up her feet and stretched out her arms, keeping her head high. The current took her. She was flying through the water. She forgot the cold; she forgot the fear. She vowed to ride this current as far north as she could, until she saw the hill the old man had told her about. On that hill, she would find the cemetery.

It was dawn when Afrika finally collapsed behind the tombstone, shivering, her teeth chattering. The last thing she remembered thinking was, looking at the marks on the stone, the letters: They had meaning. It seemed quite wondrous.

Just before her eyes closed, she thought that someday, when she was free, she'd learn how to read those letters. But right now she was mighty grateful to this dead soul, whether he be white or not, for his stone now blocked the wind which was sharp with cold.

Chapter 6
March 17, 1858
Norfolk, Virginia

"Frieda." The man would whisper, "Frieda!" But her eyes were so heavy she could not open them. On some milky border between waking and sleeping she heard them talking, their soft voices filled with a kind of wonder. Then she heard the click of the lady's shoes and a rattle of paper. "Charles." The woman's voice was suddenly crisp. "It says here, in this letter reporting on the others from whom she was separated, that although the child was commonly known as Frieda, her mother had called her Afrika."

Now they both bent over her. "Afrika!" Mrs. Page whispered. Afrika's eyes fluttered open briefly, and she smiled at the two faces above her. Then she went back to sleep again.

The next time she woke she heard them discussing another letter, one that Charles Page was composing. It seems that she was to have a new name.

"Joe Bell. Is that what she is to be called, Charles?"

"Yes. Listen to my reasoning." He then began to read the letter. This time Afrika stayed awake.

My Dear Sir:

Due to the shortage of the last shipment of Taylor Island oysters, I am willing to supplement with an additional load of Jobells, which are known for their delicacy of flavor. We must wait another week, however, to harvest the Jobells, as they are still somewhat puny in this season. I think you will have no trouble selling this lot upon arrival directly from the vessel and although you might get a higher price in Baltimore, it has been our experience that it is better to avoid the middlemen up there; thus assuring yourself a more decent profit at your own port, or if you so desire send them on to the smokehouses of our German friends.

I am sorry for this delay, but I think it only wise

to wait until these particular oysters are ready, for harvested too early they lose their sweetness.

I remain your friend,
Charles Page

He turned to look at Afrika with an intense and worried expression. She kept her eyes closed and pretended to sleep. "Lord knows," he muttered, "if these oysters will ever gain any sweetness."

For days now Afrika had slipped in and out of consciousness, but this morning a corner seemed to have been turned. The wheezing had subsided. Her breathing, which had sounded like a dull razor being stropped, had smoothed out. The fever was all but gone, yet she still seemed to suffer bouts of delirium. She talked an unintelligible babble about moon babies, dogs, and letters. She kept screaming out about letters. And then sometimes she would just moan endlessly or start repeating over and over a nonsense word that sounded like "juba."

She had been at the Page home for several days already. But now she heard them speaking again about how she must remain longer.

"Well, it's absolutely unthinkable that she will be able to leave in less than a week."

"It makes me nervous, my dear. We both know that handbills are plastered all over Norfolk advertising the fugitives from Marlymont, and there was a close description of a gap-toothed girl."

Afrika began to tremble under her covers. She slid her tongue through the gap in her teeth. Then she quickly fell into a deep, deep dream.

Soon Mammee Bert would be getting up. Then she'd feel the cold air wash over her and the other little ones cuddled against the mountains of Mammee's flesh. There were four of them altogether who slept all curled up within the warm dark landscape of the large woman's body. Afrika slept right by her calves. Her face pressed up to the back of Mammee's knees. Benny always slept against her backside. Maidee, the new girl, slept propped against her immense stomach, and then the baby, Jim, slept in Mammee Bert's arms.

Afrika had never been young enough or little enough to fit in Mammee's arms. She'd been at Talleystone for two seeding times, one harvest and one winter so far. And soon she'd be outgrowing the calves. Then she would have to get out, sleep on a corn husk pallet with another child more her size, and it would never be as warm again. Sometimes Mammee got up in the middle of the night, but that was a different kind of getting up than morning time. Not so cold. When this happened she'd gather all the little ones that slept around her together, bunching them up into a warm pile, and pull a thick cover over the whole lot. She'd go over to the farthest corner of the cabin where the potato hole was dug. She'd lift off the cover, crouch on her knees, and stick her head way down. If there were too many potatoes in it, she'd take a few out. The first time, Afrika didn't know what Mammee Bert was doing with her head down that hole, her haunches rocking back and forth. It wasn't till later that she found out that she was praying. It was her praying hole.

"What she doing?" Afrika asked Benny.

"She be praying."

"To what? Potatoes?"

"No!" Benny giggled. "It's her praying hole. Only place Mammee Bert can pray. Last time she got caught praying with them slaves from over at

Tuckeroo, they like'd to strip the flesh off Mammee Bert's back."

"They whupped Mammee Bert?"

"You bet. I sleep against that back. I know every whup mark. She got ruts in her back worse than a road in mud time."

Afrika's eyes opened wide. She stared at the rocking figure of Mammee. She couldn't believe that anyone, not Master, not anyone, would ever whup Mammee Bert. She'd seen them take slaves up to the wall, put their hands in the iron rings so they couldn't move, so their bodies pressed flat to the wall. She'd seen the flesh open up and the blood run till their backs looked like ribbons — red ribbons, the kind the mistress's little twin girls sometimes wore in their hair. She couldn't imagine Mammee Bert's beautiful plum-black skin ripped to shreds. When Mammee came back to the pallet, Afrika breathed in the fragrance of her skin, and in the darkness of the night, she found the other black — the plum-black of those swelling calves — so lovely, so warm. She loved those calves of Mammee Bert's. Master's whip hadn't reached them — they were still smooth, smooth and dark, and even on *the blackest night, Afrika could see their purple sheen. She would tuck the memory of that purple away. She'd keep it with her even when she grew too big to sleep with Mammee anymore. She'd remember it when she had to move over to that lonely pallet and share it with that bag-of-bones girl they couldn't turn into a breeder.*

No warmth there. Susu's jutting bones hurt, and her skin was always cold. When she did move over, Afrika found more warmth against the wall boards. That was when she made her discovery. The cracks between the boards were daubed with mud and clay and straw. The pallet that they slept on was in the raised part of the cabin, and one night Afrika saw a cold, sharp, white line of light, thin as a thread. She poked out some of the daub and there, perfectly framed, was a star low in the night sky. Sometimes it would be there, sometimes not, depending on the clouds and the time of year. She saw it best in the coldest months of winter. Then at fixing-fence time, which was long before seed time, it would begin to slip away.

She was pretty sure it had slipped down in the sky and not gone up because one night she snuck out to see if, like some stars, it might have climbed higher. But she could find it nowhere. If it weren't on the night's ceiling, it must be down in the night's potato hole — maybe praying, she thought, like Mammee Bert. That star might come and it might go, didn't matter, Afrika loved it, treasured it the same way she loved the purple sheen of Mammee Bert's calves. Afrika became expert in finding and loving the smallest and most fleeting things. She knew how to care for them in her mind's eye. It was too bright here now for starshine, but how come Mammee Bert wasn't getting up? Day half gone. They'll all get whupped. Oh, them terrible ribbons, she moaned.

"What's that, child?"

Afrika's eyes opened slowly. She did not speak. Experience had taught her to mind her words. She rarely spoke unless it was absolutely necessary. She blinked. Sun poured through a window, and white curtains blew softly in the breeze. Tiny, pale blue flowers seemed to grow right out of the walls. She blinked again. Did they grow, or had they been painted? And on the coverlet was a thin hand. It began patting her hand. Stroking it. She looked up.

An old woman, so white, so thin she seemed almost transparent, leaned over her. Her hairline receded, giving her forehead a bony look. Where the hair began, it was thin and white as goose down. Her eyes were a fierce blue, and her nose was beaked. "I thought you'd never come 'round, child. I must call you Joe. You remember that, don't you? You are Joe Bell."

"Joe Bell." Afrika moved her lips around the two words. Why did she know those words?

"Are you hungry? I have a bowl with some corn bread broken up in warm milk. I can feed you a bit."

Then the frail woman reached over and put her arm around Afrika, lifting her up while she spooned some of the sopped bread into her mouth. Afrika knew about spoons. White people in the great house always ate with them, and so did some of the house slaves, but she had never had a spoon in her mouth. She wasn't sure if she liked it or not. She thought maybe the food tasted better from her fingers.

"Tell me," the woman said after she had spooned in several mouthfuls. "Do you know how old you are?" There was no answer. "Do you remember how many harvest times or planting times . . ." Her voice dwindled off, and she sighed. Afrika was asleep again, but this time it was not the troubled sleep of fever. This time she slept peacefully.

Maidee swung her little hips next to Afrika at the trough as she dug her oyster shell into the cornmeal mush. "Juba this and Juba that," she sang in a high, thin whine. All that child did was sing since she'd come. But when she wasn't singing she was crying, so Afrika guessed this was better. The girl would get used to it. Afrika had gotten used to it, she supposed. Mammee Bert, who took care of the young ones, was good to them. She could be strict and give them a whup, but she didn't waste any whups. She only did it if she thought the master or mistress would deliver worse. She was always very clear about that when she whupped them.

"Look!" Afrika nudged the hip-swaying girl with her elbow. "You singing so hard you missed that piece of pork!" She'd scooped up the piece for Maidee. "You don't get pork in here but maybe once in a long while. You better stop all that juba business right now else you going to starve."

Maidee stopped her singing and looked carefully at Afrika. *She don't trust me,* Afrika thought. *She'd seen that look before. She thinks I'm up to no good. And if she knows all about not trusting and no good, what she doing crying here at Talleystone — maybe this place be better than where she came from?* She dug in again to the warm cornmeal mush with her shell. *This is stupid. How can I be eating when I feel so warm and soft like I be in bed?*

Chapter 7

April 1858

Norfolk, Virginia

Now child, Captain Briggs will sail you up the Chesapeake to a point directly across from Cove Point Lighthouse."

Charles Page spoke each word clearly, and Afrika had never listened so carefully in her life. It seemed more complicated than anything she had done so far. If she could have gone directly to Baltimore, it would have been a simpler and more direct route to the free states. But there were patrollers, slave catchers, swarming around the major ports these days. Just getting out of Norfolk would be dangerous.

"He's got a shallow-draft boat, and if the coast is clear he'll duck into the Little Choptank River, just south of Cambridge. You must follow the Little Choptank north and east until it joins with the

Choptank. This is a distance of no more than ten miles. So it is not too far.

"You'll know you're approaching the Choptank when the Little Choptank begins to peter out. It's pretty near to dry at the end. There'll be some marsh right before the Choptank. You must then follow the Choptank. This is a distance of fifty miles, at least. The going is not easy. It will take you three or four days. There are no stations along the Choptank. It is wooded all the way. At the end, the water narrows to a trickle, then you have to come out of the woods and head for Camden. It is another fifteen miles.

"There is a big open field. You will have to do it at night, Joe Bell. About a mile beyond the church on the main road into Camden there is a cabin. There is a free Negro there who works for Ezekiel Hunn. Mr. Hunn is the stationmaster for Camden, but you take your directions on how to find his house and how to approach it from this free Negro lady."

They left later that same night. Afrika was a boy again — this time Joe Bell, in a new pair of pants that fit much better and a handsome jacket that

Dorothy Page had made herself. She had squared off the shoulders and put in large pads so that Afrika's slender frame suddenly acquired more masculine proportions. She carried a satchel filled with bread, several thick slabs of cheese, and a pork end. She even wore a cravat.

Captain Briggs was waiting with his full load of oysters — ten barrels, in addition to four barrels for crabs.

"I didn't know you crabbed, Captain," Charles Page said in a tight voice.

"I reckon I take anything I kin catch, friend," Briggs replied. "Smith Island up the bay is rich in crabs. I got me traps there. Them crabs are a lot lighter to rest under than oysters, if you get my meaning." He looked quickly at the Pages and then at Afrika. Afrika got his meaning. The Pages had explained to her how at any time, particularly during the day, Briggs might throw her into a barrel with oysters if other watermen approached.

"Well, we best be off. No moon tonight. Dark as pitch. I be most happy, miss, if you'd climb into that barrel there right now. We're still close to Norfolk, and I fetched those crabs specially up at Smith's for just this purpose."

Afrika removed her new coat and carefully folded the plum cravat into the pocket. Dorothy Page watched her with tears. Afrika took one last look at the Pages. "Thank you," she whispered, but she could hardly form the words. She then climbed into the deep barrel.

"Fold yourself up now. You might want to tie that cravat over your face or hold your hands up to protect yourself, but these crabs don't really pinch."

"Sir," she said suddenly. "How 'bout that screen over there?" She pointed to a circle of mesh resting on top of another barrel.

"What about it?"

"Would it fit in here? You put that on top after I climb in, then the crabs on top of that. And they can't get at me."

"I'll be!" Briggs took off his cap and scratched his head. "I never thought of that. Now it won't fit into this barrel, but it fits into that there bait barrel. No bait in it, but it stinks to high heaven. If you can stand that?"

"Yes, sir." She nodded.

"Cover your scent real good, these here Johnny

Macks." The captain's voice was filled with surprise.

Afrika hitched a leg over the barrel's edge and then crunched down inside. It sure did stink. There was a squeak and then scraping sounds as he fitted in the screen.

Captain Briggs spoke. "Don't worry, it won't be for long. As soon as we clear the light off Norfolk, we'll get you out."

"You going to have to call me Johnny Mack instead of Joe Bell." Afrika looked up at him.

The captain bent low until his face was just inches from her own and only separated by the mesh of the screen. "I'm going to call you smart!"

Afrika looked up through the mesh. She could still see the sky with a scattering of stars. Then there was a soft thud, and a piece of the sky disappeared. Afrika felt her heart beat faster. More thuds, a scraping sound, and another part of the night vanished. Soon the last glimmer of the last star was swallowed by a hissing, moving tangle of claws. The crabs kept coming. Layer upon layer of them. Afrika's breath grew rapid and shallow. She closed her eyes, squeezing them tight until she saw red squiggles and sparks exploding on the inside of her eyelids.

When she opened her eyes, she did not see the snaggle of claws. She didn't feel the dripping saltwater on her cheeks. Instead her mind was filled with the kindness of Dorothy Page. She thought about the shape of the bony forehead and the curious deep blue eyes. Mrs. Page had a purple vein that came up across her temple. Afrika liked that, too. It reminded her of that other purple from a long time ago, the plum sheen at the heart of Mammee Bert's blackness.

Chapter 8

April 1858

Boston, Massachusetts

I t was more of a crack than a snap. Every time
they jibed the sloop, Lucy looked up to see if
the mast on *Winsome* had splintered.

"You're coming to it, child." Her grandfather
grinned out from under the sou'wester hat.

When they had started out, the sun had been
shining, but it soon clouded up, and a drizzle
began. A fine mist it was, accompanied by a
steadily increasing breeze, perfect for honing
the skills necessary in handling a sloop like the
Winsome. Lucy sailed as Pap had taught her,
with a chart in one hand and her eye on the
compass. Pap had explained the difference between the true north of the chart, which was
oriented toward geographic north, and the mag-
netic north indicated by the compass. The dif-

ference here in Massachusetts Bay was almost seventeen degrees.

Pap was putting Lucy through her paces. They had tacked out of the harbor, and it had taken them more than an hour to reach Boston Light. Once there, Pap had her tack back and forth between the lighthouse and Shag Rocks. And now he wanted her to intentionally jibe.

This was tricky. More than one sailor had been seriously injured or even killed by the crack of a jibing boom. She had to do it right.

"Let's try it again, Luce," her grandfather said. "Get up a head of steam so we can really jibe."

The narrow hull of *Winsome* sliced through the gray choppy waters of Massachusetts Bay. They ran down for another two minutes.

"All right, Pap. Sheet in."

Pap then turned his attention to the mainsail.

"Get set. Jibe ho!" she called and pushed the wheel hard to starboard. The boom snapped across.

"Bravo!" Pap applauded. "You see, Lucy, you were rightly named. You've got just the right touch. But it's time for us to head back, what with the big do at the Adamses' tonight. Your mother is going to want to get you quite dressed up, this being your first grown-up party."

"Rot!" muttered Lucy. But she knew he was right. It wouldn't do to be late, else her mother wouldn't let her out sailing again. Ever since her last birthday, when she turned fourteen, Pap always let her be the captain. This was the one place in the whole world where it didn't seem to matter that she had been born a girl. "All right, Pap, ease off on the main and the jib. We can run down wing and wing."

The two sails billowed out on either side of *Winsome*'s cream-colored hull, and she took off downwind like a water sprite. Great sweeping arcs of spray flew off the hull.

"It's a Nantucket sleigh ride," bellowed her grandfather over the wind. But to Lucy it felt as if she were riding on the back of an immense angel, a saltwater angel made of stick and string and beautifully crafted wood with wings of sea spray and canvas.

Two hours later, Lucy stood glowering at her reflection in the long, oval looking glass. It was not just the hideous color of the dress — a bilious yellow. She could endure only so much for this wedding. And one thing she could not stand was being dressed like an idiot.

In addition to its vile color, the dress was flounced. Lucy hated flounces. They got in the way. If you looked silly to begin with, they made you look sillier. If you were smart, they made you look dumb. The only thing Lucy hated more than flounces was when women wore dead birds on their hats. Mrs. Forbes had attended Symphony Hall with a complete golden finch, dead as a doornail, perched on the brim of her latest hat. She would probably be at the party tonight in one of her creations from Paris.

Most Boston ladies left their gowns wrapped in tissue paper for a year before wearing them. It was considered proper restraint. But Lucy's mother had decided to take out her dress six months early. For after all, as she explained, when she had bought it she had no idea that there would be an engagement party in April.

This was the first of many grand events leading up to Iris and Elwyn's wedding. The Van Schuylers were up from New York in full force, and there was even a scattering of their southern relatives from New Orleans. After all her years of enduring "cold roast Boston," Lucy's mother was beside herself with excitement. This union would bring New Yorkers and a precious few Southerners into the family. She hoped there might be one or two eligible young men for Rose, Daisy, or Delphinia.

Lucy continued to glower at her reflection.

"What are you making that terrible face at, Lucy?" Delphinia Bradford came through the door in a rustle of watered silk.

"Myself. Who do you think?"

"Why, in heaven's name?" Delphinia slid an arm around her younger sister. "You look positively grown-up. You should be so happy. How many fourteen-year-olds get to go to an evening party?"

"Nobody will listen to me in this stupid dress. They'll think I'm dying or too silly to have a thought."

"Lucy, mark my words." Delphinia looked her younger sister straight in the eye. "No one will ever think that of you." She gave her a squeeze.

Daisy stuck her head in the room. "What's wrong with Lucy? Glum again?"

"She doesn't like her dress. Thinks it makes her look ill."

"Lucy always looks ill. Has ever since the engagement was announced. I've never seen such a poor sport. I think she's jealous."

"Oh, Daisy," Delphinia gasped. "Really you are too much. Your remarks are absolutely cruel."

"I'm just sick of her carrying on, that's all." Daisy turned and walked out the door.

"I'm going to speak to Mama," Lucy said fiercely. "I'm going to ask her if I can wear the periwinkle blue that I wore in Newport last summer. It's warm enough."

"I wish you well!"

Lucy walked reluctantly now down the hall to her mother's dressing room. Maybe she should wear the awful dress and be done with it. As she approached the double doors, she could hear people talking. Her father was in the room.

"It's not that I'm saying no to the liveried footmen and the silk stockings, but you have to admit, Emeralda, it's not quite Boston, and what will Father say?"

"Nothing fun is ever Boston, and as for your father, well, he would probably be happiest if the wedding took place in that decrepit old Unitarian church, and the bridesmaids wore home spun and starched caps."

"Now that's simply not true, and you know it, Emeralda. He sent over several magnums of champagne as a gift for the party at the Adamses' tonight. He is thrilled about Iris and Elwyn."

"Oh, dear Lord, I do hope that the Adamses don't serve the usual."

"Now what do you mean by that?"

"You know, a boiled fowl, overcooked vegetables, and, oh, Sherbourne, you don't think they'll have Indian pudding, not for a festive occasion like this?"

"Of course not, darling. Don't be ridiculous."

"And good heavens, Sherbourne, you don't think there will be any abolitionist nonsense being discussed?"

"Of course not. This is an engagement celebration."

"But some of them are on that fool Vigilance Committee, I just know it. And if they aren't on it, they have close ties to it and the Free Soilers."

"Emeralda." A sharp tone crept into his voice.

"Do not think that only Southerners know how to behave on such occasions. Some of us Bostonians may have abolitionist sympathies, but we are mannered. We do not discuss this sort of thing at dinner parties. And as you know, six years ago we agreed never to discuss these issues in our family.

"I'll tell you right now, dear, many of our friends' and relatives' liberal sympathies are going right out the window as they contemplate the future of their mills without a good steady flow of cotton. I know for a fact that Appleton and Amory are fit to be tied about all this. They stand to lose quite a bit with their mills."

It was at this juncture in the conversation that Lucy decided to knock.

"Yes?"

"Mama," Lucy said as she entered.

"My, don't you look all grown-up!" her father exclaimed. He rose from the chaise longue and gave a small bow.

"Oh, you look glorious, Lucy," her mother cried. "That color is marvelous on you. It subdues your complexion, yet does not overpower."

"Oh, mother!" Lucy moaned.

Both parents' faces puckered in sudden concern. "What is it, Lucy dear?" Her father came
and put his arm around her. Just his touch was too
much. Suddenly tears were spilling down her
cheeks.

"Oh dear! Don't spot your dress," Emeralda
fussed.

"Here, here." Lucy's father drew out a large
handkerchief.

"She must be nervous about her first grown-up
party. There's nothing to be nervous about, Lucy."

Then words came out in a garbled flood.

"What dying?" her father repeated. "Who's
dying?"

"I said I look like I'm dying in this color."

"Nonsense," said her mother.

"You look glorious," said her father.

"I look like bile!"

"Don't say such an awful word, Lucy," whispered her mother.

"It's not an awful word. It's a brownish-yellow
liquid secreted by the liver. . . ."

"Lucy!" Her mother shrieked. "Oh, Sherbourne, she's absolutely freakish."

"This dress is freakish. I hate it, Mama. Do I have to wear it? You know I never liked the color. Couldn't I wear the periwinkle?"

There was a silence. Lucy's father looked anxiously at his wife. "Couldn't she, Emeralda?"

"But if we let her do this, then she'll object to something about the bridesmaid dress, and that can't be changed because she is part of a procession, and all the colors must blend."

"I promise, Mama, I won't object. I promise. I'll wear anything you tell me to the wedding. I'll wear any color if it is part of the plan of the wedding. I promise, but this is my first grown-up party, and couldn't I?"

Emeralda looked at her youngest daughter in confusion. Lucy thought her mother loved her, she guessed she did, but neither one understood the other in the least.

"All right, Lucy, if it will make you happy. You have done a very nice job on that last set of tea towels."

"Oh, Mama." Lucy ran to embrace her. The ruby at her mother's throat dug into her cheek.

"And, Lucy dear," her father said, "I nearly forgot." From his waistcoat pocket he drew a small box. "When Mother and I were in Paris I bought you something for your next birthday, but since Mother is not waiting to wear her new gown, and since we both agree that you really have been a good sport recently about all this wedding business, well, we'd like to give this to you on the occasion of your first grown-up party."

"For me." Lucy took the satin box and stared at it. The jeweler's name was inscribed on the cover in gold writing.

"Go on, open it!" Emeralda urged.

Lucy lifted the lid. "Oh! It's beautiful!" It was a pin. A soft explosion of blossoms made from a dozen perfect pearls burst from a delicate filigree of gold fashioned to look like stems and leaves.

"Now quickly dear, go change your dress. Delphy can help you fasten the pin."

Chapter 9

April 1858

Boston, Massachusetts

Thirty minutes later, the Bradfords set out for the home of Charles Francis and Abigail Adams at 57 Mount Vernon. They took two carriages, Mr. and Mrs. Bradford in the first one with the betrothed couple, and the four other daughters in the second. Daisy, Delphinia, and Rose patted their hair, smoothed their dresses, and arranged their various wraps incessantly during the short ride. But Lucy sat perfectly still. She was wearing the periwinkle blue dress, no flounces, just a deep border of embroidered butterflies. The beautiful new pin was perfect with the butterflies. She felt fine, even pretty.

"I wonder if Wendell Phillips will be there," Delphinia said.

"Never!" said Daisy. "He's an agitator. There is

not a house on Beacon Hill that would open its door to him. Papa says he's a worse rabble-rouser than William Lloyd Garrison."

"His father was Wendell Phillips, president of Harvard," Delphinia added.

"Doesn't matter what his father was," Rose snapped. "His manners are terrible."

"It's not his manners," Daisy said coolly. "It's his beliefs."

"I find him quite attractive."

"Delphy!" Rose cried. "He's old enough to be your father."

"What about cousin Francis Parkman?" Lucy said.

"Much better choice," Rose added.

"Though his health leaves something to be desired," Daisy offered.

"Well, Daisy." Delphinia spoke softly while looking out the carriage window. "You shouldn't discourage me, or I might have to turn my attention to some of Elwyn's gentlemen cousins I've been hearing about."

Daisy shot her sister a look of absolute venom.

Lucy could hardly believe that mild Delphy would ever dare to bait Daisy like this.

*   *   *

The carriage pulled up in front of 57 Mount Vernon. The first thing Lucy did as she entered the main parlor was to look for her grandfather.

"Who are you looking for so intently?" Rose asked.

"Pap. Is he here yet?"

"Ooh, Lucy, don't say Pap. It will upset Mama. She says that's what the little pickaninnies call the old Negro men down on the plantations in the South."

"Well, I'm not a little pickaninny, and this isn't a plantation in the South. Pap is what I've called him since ever I can remember. Grandmother was Pup, and to me it made sense to call him Pap."

"Oh, Lucy, you are so stubborn. Do grow up."

"Sisters!" Elwyn came over to them both and kissed them on their cheeks. Once on each cheek, which made for four kisses in all. New Yorkers kissed a lot, Lucy decided. But she did like Elwyn. "You both look radiant. And Lucy, I thoroughly approve of your gown." He dropped his voice. "It's much better, I'm sure, than the bile one."

"You know?" Lucy flushed.

"Of course. But I think you were absolutely right."

Lucy thought Elwyn was such a good sport, and he always knew the right thing to say to make everyone feel comfortable. He never ever made her feel like the baby sister.

"Lucy dear!" A voice like honey oozed through the throngs. Oh no! It was Aunt Opal. "My word, chile, all grown-up and at your first grown-up party!"

Aunt Opal had a knack for saying the most irritating things, but they seemed less irritating because of her Southern accent. Of all of Lucy's aunts, Aunt Opal had the deepest accent.

There were more kisses all around for Opal and Mrs. Van Schuyler, who was by her side.

Lucy decided to slip off amidst all the kissing. She slid behind two gentlemen standing nearby. They did not seem to notice her.

"Now remember, Edmund" — the voice was low and confidential — "this is Boston, the home, no less, of Charles Francis Adams, member of the Free Soil party, leading abolitionist. So do not expect a lavish table. No caviar here. They pride themselves on thin broth and boiled cod."

"Really, Henry, is that all you think about? Food?" The other gentleman said this with a mild note of shock underlying his distinctly Southern drawl.

Lucy was more than shocked. It had to be the height of ill manners to criticize the hosts while in their home. She was standing behind the man who had offered his opinion of the Adamses' table. He was portly, and his neck was pink, swine pink, with rolls of fat bulging over his collar.

"So where are the lovely sisters?" the man with the drawl asked.

"Well, there framed in the door is one. I believe that's Rose. Quite delectable — all of them, really. Ummmm."

Lucy's stomach turned.

"And aah . . . there's the other . . . Daisy. Lovely, *n'est-ce pas*?" Dear Lord! The man was practically slurping.

"Charming . . . charming . . ." the other man drawled and craned his neck for a better glimpse.

"And with fortunes to match, Edmund. There's

a younger one, too, much younger. Thirteen or fourteen."

"Well, we shan't rob the cradle, now, shall we, Henry?"

Indeed! Lucy felt the blood pound in her temples. It was all she could do not to shout out loud and deliver a swift kick in the pants to these two deplorable men. Especially the fat one.

"Are you all right?" a voice next to her inquired. She turned her head.

"Oh!" Lucy inhaled sharply. The earnest eyes registered concern.

"I mean, is it too warm in here? You look rather — well — frankly, red."

"Oh, don't worry. I just get that way sometimes." She could not help but keep looking into his eyes. They were deep set and crinkled slightly at the corners. His face was a lean, hawkish one.

The young man leaned forward a bit. There was a sudden sparkle in his eye. "Aren't you one of the Bradford sisters? Lucy, right?"

She had barely said yes when the two gentlemen whose disturbing conversation had nearly caused her to ignite wheeled about.

"Ah! A sister of the bride." The fat man spoke.

Lucy could smell the pomade he had applied liberally to the little flattened ringlets that led down the sides of his face. He looked like a pig.

His friend was quite the opposite — thin, with jet-black hair that swept straight back from a high, prominent forehead. His eyes were a pale, almost translucent brown.

"Permit us to introduce ourselves. I'm Henry Van Schuyler," the plump man said.

"And I'm Edmund de Rosey."

"We're both cousins of the groom."

"I'm Lucy Bradford," Lucy said.

"And I'm Robert Shaw," said the man Lucy had first been talking to.

"Robert Shaw!" Lucy exclaimed. "Of course. I remember, out in Dedham . . ."

"Yes, and we'd never let you play croquet. But we would now, rest assured. Do you want to play today? I'm sure Uncle Charles wouldn't mind." He laughed merrily. His face was wonderful when he laughed, creased with true pleasure. There was something very genuine about Robert Shaw.

"Are we cousins?" Lucy asked suddenly. And then she really did blush deeply, but Shaw didn't seem to notice.

"Probably, most everybody here is. Are you related to the Parkmans?" he asked.

"Yes, of course."

"Well, then, we are."

"I say," interjected Henry Van Schuyler. "Is that Francis Parkman — the Oregon Trail chap?"

"Indeed!" said Lucy. "We're all quite proud of him."

"You're a Harvard man, right?" Van Schuyler asked as he turned to Shaw.

"Yes," Shaw answered. "Class of 1860. Two more years to go."

"Once a Harvard man, always a Harvard man. Isn't that how it goes?" Van Schuyler continued.

Edmund de Rosey cleared his throat somewhat nervously. It was clear to Lucy that de Rosey was not completely comfortable with his cousin's manners.

"For some, perhaps," Shaw replied cryptically.

At just that moment, Iris came up with both Rose and Daisy. "Cousin Henry and Cousin Edmund, you must meet my sisters Rose and Daisy."

Lucy turned to Shaw. "I think it's about time for some croquet, Robert."

"By all means."

Giving a coquettish cough as she passed by Henry Van Schuyler, Lucy swirled open her small fan and whispered to him, "Now we shan't have to rob the cradle!"

In a far corner of the room, Lucy turned to Shaw. "I found those two gentlemen revolting."

Shaw blinked in astonishment, and Lucy related the conversation she had overheard.

"You know, Lucy, I completely agree with you. If I were a young lady, yes, I think I would find that revolting. But . . ." He hesitated.

"What is it?" Lucy asked.

"Well, if you don't mind me saying, you're quite different from most girls I've met."

"I expect so," Lucy said matter-of-factly. "My mother says I'm absolutely freakish."

"She does?"

"Yes."

"Does that disturb you?"

Now it was Lucy's turn to pause. No one had ever asked her such a question, and she was not sure what she felt.

"Well." She spoke slowly. "I am what I am, and yes, I think it would be much nicer, less strange, you know, to fit in, but . . . but. . . ." She felt Shaw watching her closely. "But I suppose mostly it makes me sad that the world must name its freaks at all — that there is such a thing as freakish when to me it feels normal. It is simply my nature after all, not intended."

A bell tinkled, and the Adamses' ancient family butler, Benton, opened the double doors leading from the parlor into the dining room. As they streamed through, Lucy spotted her grandfather absorbed in conversation with William Appleton. "So where's old Amory?" she heard her grandfather ask.

"Savannah, where I should be, Lev, making sure we're going to have a supply of cotton for our mills — what with the leakage."

Lucy saw the muscles in her grandfather's jaw clench.

Franklin Sanborn, standing on the other side of Appleton, coughed slightly. "I take it, William, you are referring to the fugitive-slave situation."

"It's not a situation. It is a condition that would better be described as a hemorrhage. And it's going to bleed us all."

Levi Bradford remained stonily silent. Business and politics were never discussed in mixed company. The time for that would come after dinner, when the women withdrew to the drawing room and the men took their brandy and cigars separately in the library with their host. Franklin Sanborn adjusted his cravat and walked briskly into the dining room.

Lucy was disappointed not to be seated anywhere near Shaw, but to her relief she was not near the dreadful Henry Van Schuyler. She felt herself lucky, really, for she was near Elwyn and right next to her grandfather. The table was beautifully set, and in the center were silver bowls with sprays of white violets imported from the Adamses' greenhouses on their estate in Quincy.

"Never been to one of these dos before, Luce?" Levi Bradford whispered the question in her ear.

"Never. I hope I do it right."

"Don't worry. Follow me." He patted her hand softly.

The first course was oxtail soup. This was followed by grilled cod cheeks.

"First-rate cod cheeks," Levi Bradford muttered. "I doubt, though, if the New Yorkers will take to them."

Between this course and the next there was a terrapin, something that the New Yorkers were more familiar with, for there was much talk about sea turtles versus freshwater. After the terrapin, Charles Francis Adams rose to toast the betrothed couple with champagne.

"And I might add that as marvelous as it is to be able to toast this wonderful young couple, we have four other equally charming Bradford girls here at the table. And if their grandfather continues to supply us with champagne for each one of their betrothals, he shall destroy our reputation for plain living and high thinking."

Levi Bradford rose to answer the toast. He liked nothing better than sparring with his old friend.

"Well, dear friend, what the champagne did to destroy our reputation for plain living, the cod cheeks will certainly restore." There was a burst of raucous laughter at this. He continued his toast, which was a delicate blend of wit and sensibility.

Lucy basked in the sunshine of the laughter that her grandfather had provoked. Would she ever have the words or the grace to say such funny and charming things? Of course, women never gave toasts, so there would never be such an occasion.

The dinner continued. There was no Indian pudding for dessert, but ice cream molded into beautiful flowers.

Just after the dessert was set down, Lucy noticed Benton approach Mrs. Adams, lean down, and whisper something in her ear. She saw Mrs. Adams smile and then direct him to her grandfather.

"Sir, Mrs. Adams wishes me to thank you for the dates. Your housekeeper just dropped them by and said she knew you had hoped they would get here in time for dessert or at least coffee. They shall be served."

"Oh." Levi's bushy white eyebrows shot up. He coughed. "You say they just arrived?"

"Yes, sir. Your serving girl, or rather housekeeper — Zephyra I believe is her name — brought them over herself."

"Capital! Capital!"

*   *   *

Immediately following dessert, Charles and Abigail Adams rose to lead their guests from the dining room. Lucy saw her grandfather quickly seek out Charles. Was something wrong? She noticed a look of concern on Charles's face. Yes, and her grandfather was limping a bit. Not his gout again! But she was soon caught in the flow of ladies streaming into the drawing room, where card tables had already been set up.

Before the ladies had all settled, she slipped out into the hall.

"Benton," she called. The elderly servant was just going into the library with a decanter of brandy on a tray with glasses.

"Yes, miss?"

"My grandfather, Dr. Bradford."

"Oh, don't worry, miss. Just a touch of the gout, he said. He especially didn't want any of his family to worry. Said Jeremy, his coachman, 'could haul his old bones home.' I believe those were the words."

"Oh," said Lucy. "Thank you."

Benton continued into the library with his tray. Lucy looked in after him. She would much prefer to be in the library with the gentlemen. She knew that in the drawing room, the conversation would be unmitigated wedding talk. How nice if someone became unmannered and began to discuss the fugitive-slave law or abolition. She peeked into the drawing room. On the swirling eddies of conversation she heard the trill of her mother's voice holding forth on the subject of trousseaus. Lucy simply could not face it.

She turned and wandered into another little drawing room, where a very elderly aunt of Abigail Adams snored softly in a rocker by the coal grate. On a nearby table was a snifter of brandy filled with a rather stout amount for such a frail-looking thing. Perhaps Lucy would stay in here for just a minute or two. No one would notice.

She walked over to the deep bayed window. Moonlight drifted down on the narrow cobbled street, making the air look like silver dust. To her left, she could see a familiar figure walking quickly down toward Charles Street. And there was not a trace of a limp! "Pap!" Lucy whispered.

A few moments later, another figure appeared just outside the window, unmistakable in its bulk. Henry Van Schuyler! He clutched his stovepipe hat in his hands as if he had not had time to place it on his head. He looked up the street and down. Then he ran his fingers through his carefully oiled hair in a gesture of frustration.

Lucy looked again toward the foot of Mount Vernon. There was no trace of her grandfather. Henry Van Schuyler headed in the opposite direction, the only direction that carriages were permitted to go on the steep, narrow street.

Lucy was totally confounded. Why had her grandfather left the party if, indeed, he was not suffering from gout? And if he were suffering, how had he recovered so quickly? He was fairly springing down Mount Vernon Street. And Henry Van Schuyler — what was his excuse? It was considered terribly rude to leave a party this early. Was he sick, too? What was he looking for? Why had he been clutching his hat so frantically? None of this made any sense to Lucy.

Yet at this very moment, Lucy had a sudden sharp sense that the fact that she did not understand was irrelevant; that perhaps there was another condition far more significant. Perhaps there were powers and forces operating that would affect every person, every dust mote in this house, and perhaps no one understood these powers any better than she did. And it wouldn't matter whether bombazine was chosen for a trousseau gown or whether the banking rates went up or down. Perhaps it was all just talk and all as meaningless as the old lady's snoring in the face of these invisible powers. Lucy turned and went back into the drawing room. Mrs. Cabot was holding forth on an article she had read concerning the healthful ventilation of rooms involving something called "the disinfecting principle."

Chapter 10
April 10, 1858

Chesapeake Bay, south of Taylor Island

off the eastern shore of Maryland

Afrika pulled the jacket tighter and tipped her face toward the stars. If it could only go on like this forever. But come first light she would have to climb back into the barrel with the crabs.

Well, one thing was certain — she must reek of those Johnny Macks and the crabs. No slave dog would pick up her scent. Captain Briggs said he had something special for her to give them if they did. Called it a hush puppy. Looked just like a finger of corn bread. But he said he'd laced it with poison, and a dog would drop dead in its tracks before it could get a nip at a fugitive. She hoped it wouldn't come to that. But she knew there was a hard stretch ahead.

For now, though, she was content. The North Star blazed in the deep velvety black vault of the sky. The soft Chesapeake breeze stroked her ears and neck. The lap of the waves against the skip-jack's hull was like a saltwater lullaby. She had never been more at peace, more comfortable, not even in Mrs. Page's big feather bed. If she could take this boat all the way to Canada, she would. But Captain called it flat bottom and shoal draft. Said it was only suited for the shallow waters of the bay, for going after oysters and crabs. He said it would be smashed by the Atlantic.

"This breeze has picked up, Afrika," Captain Briggs said as he leaned against the tiller. The worn white sail billowed with the following breeze like a smudged angel in the night. "We might get there too early."

"Too early, Captain? Freedom ain't going to come too early for me."

"I'm not letting you off in broad daylight, child. If it's daylight, it's back in the barrel, and we're going to poke around Taylor Island till dark. Understand they got plenty of nice Jobell oysters up there." He chuckled.

They got along all right, she thought. When she was coming out of the barrel this evening, her shirt had hiked up, and he'd seen the scars, like a dark embroidery scrawled across her narrow back. She saw him flinch. It surprised her. If he'd been helping fugitive slaves he must have seen the bullwhip marks on a black back before. But she could tell from the look in his eye and the way he swallowed he was feeling a queasiness deep in his gut, and it wasn't seasickness.

"You be wondering about my scars." It was a statement, not a question.

"They look bad, like they done laid your back wide open."

"That they did. They had the whipping man do it 'cause I wouldn't lay no more with the overseer." She saw the color drain out of Briggs's face. "They dug a hole for my belly in the ground."

"W-w-what?" he stammered. She could tell that he didn't understand.

"They didn't want to hurt the baby in there. They ain't just raising tobacco and cotton, they breeding slaves. They can sell 'em. Babies most dependable crop of all." She spoke matter-of-factly.

"What happened to the baby?"

"Lost it. Got born early when I set out with Miss Harriet."

"That how you got separated from Moses? Heard you had."

She nodded silently. She didn't feel like talking.

Captain Briggs looked almost sick. Well, she couldn't help that. She walked up to the bow of the skipjack and let him be alone with his thoughts. And even though she pulled her jacket around her and grabbed a blanket to wear across her shoulders, she could feel him looking straight through to the scars on her back.

After a while, Afrika looked over her shoulder at the captain. He was a short, burly man with a thick red beard. He wore his cap down low, but sometimes when he pushed it up a bit she saw a small scar, jagged like a lightning streak, above his left eyebrow. She liked the way he leaned into the tiller. It was as if he were part of the boat. And she noticed that despite his thickset body, he seemed to feel every wind almost before it came and anticipate every change in the current, every angle of the waves. He was a water thing, she thought.

Captain Briggs had told her that sailors on the water could figure out their whereabouts by looking at the stars, and not only the North Star either.

He had explained that the North one was the steady one, but that the others paraded around, not any which way, but in what he called an "orderly pattern." According to Captain Briggs, depending on the time of year and what stars were showing, you could figure out exactly where you were on earth.

Afrika remembered that star she had treasured through the chink in the daub between the boards of the cabin at Talleystone. How sometimes it would be there and other times not. Made her feel good to think that even when it hadn't been there, it might have been helping some sailor on a far-away sea. Still, it sounded unbelievable to Afrika, and she was glad that she only had to keep her eye on one star, and when that one was gone behind clouds, she could feel for moss. Someday, she would know how to keep all the other stars and their movements in her head. Captain said you needed to know arithmetic, probably letters, too. Someday, she'd know letters.

"Okay, Afrika." Captain crouched a bit and squinted under the boom. "I see the loom of Taylor Island over there. It's coming up faster than I thought. We're going to have to duck in there, child, till tomorrow evening."

"All right, Captain." My goodness, Afrika thought, had she ever trusted any white person before? She supposed she had trusted the Pages. She looked up at the star-bright sky and whispered four words: "I trust you, Captain." And she thought how she trusted the stars even though she could not always see them, and she trusted the wind even though Captain said he'd seen hurricanes pull trees up by their roots, and she trusted the water even though she knew it could boil with rage. And she trusted this captain who seemed wrapped in the wind and felt the pulse of the current and knew the rhyme of the stars and the rhythm of the sea.

Chapter 11
April 1858

Mouth of the Little Choptank,

eastern Maryland

Captain Briggs nosed the skipjack into the tall reeds. "All right now. We're in luck. I got up here a further piece than I thought I could. You only going to have to follow the Little Choptank for two hours or so, no more. Then you'll come to the Big Chop. You got Mr. and Mrs. Page's directions straight?"

She had climbed out onto the narrow bank. He was knee deep in the water, ready to push the boat back out into the deeper water.

"Yes, sir, I got them directions all fixed tight in my head."

"I bet you do." Captain Briggs pressed his lips together into something like a smile. His eyes twinkled brightly. "Now don't you worry about this here little bit of rain. You won't need no

North Star if you keep Big Chop river to your left. You know you'll be heading north." He paused. "And Afrika, you got them hush puppies?"

"Yes, sir."

"Well, keep them dry. Then the poison won't leak out, and if them dogs get near, just give them one. It'll kill a dog in thirty seconds flat."

Afrika put the hush puppies in a small canvas sack the Captain had given to her.

"Look here, I can tie it right onto me inside this jacket. Then I won't lose it when I'm running."

He had turned his back as she fiddled with the small canvas sack. "Well, if you run as good as you think, you going to be free soon, Joe Bell. All right now, you better get on your way." But he didn't turn around to speak the words.

She waited a moment, hoping he would turn, but he was busy pushing the skipjack back into the deeper water.

"Captain?"

"Yes, Joe?" He turned and looked at her coldly now. "Time for you to go, Joe Bell. You get on your way quick now." He would hardly look at her.

"Well, thank you, Captain," she said just as quickly and disappeared into the brush.

Captain was right, there was no time to lose. Already she realized that she was moving too slowly. After only a couple of miles, she felt her legs shaking with their own weariness. This had never happened to her before. It took her longer than she had expected to reach Big Chop, but at least by that time the rain had stopped.

The jacket Mrs. Page had given her shed the water well. Afrika wasn't hungry, but after an hour of walking alongside Big Chop, she forced herself to sit down and take a rest and have a bite of cheese.

She still had a lot of the food Mrs. Page had given her, because Captain Briggs had shared his food with her. And with every snack, he shucked a few oysters for her to eat raw, though he said they were mighty good fried.

Funny how Captain had called her Joe Bell right at the end. She'd never much thought about being named Afrika before. She wondered why her mother had called her that. She had such a dim memory of her mother. Her face was all mixed up with the one in the dream, the one pouring blood and crawling with tobacco worms. Now that's strange. She never had caught herself thinking about that dream when she was awake. She shook herself. No way she was going to fall asleep. Her legs might be weary, but she better not sleep yet. She got up and started walking.

Her muscles had cramped up on her, and walking was harder than before. But she had to keep moving. No time for sleep. No time for dreams. The sky cleared off. Through the tangled branches, she could see it, the North Star, burning bright. *That ain't no dream,* she thought. *It might be a million miles away, but it ain't no dream.*

Afrika plunged deeper into the thick woods along the Choptank. Briers tore at her clothes, a thorny branch scratched her cheek. With her tongue she shoved the little piece of bone Mr. Page had carved for her gap further up between her teeth.

"You forget those aching legs," she yelled at herself silently. "You got to be Joe Bell now. You got strong, hard legs, hard as any big field hand."

Afrika thanked God when she saw the first pink streaks of dawn through the black branches. She knew that her legs could not have carried her another step. In front of her grew a maple tree with spreading roots. She'd dig herself a hole, like the ones that Mammee Bert got caught in at Tuckeroo, and the ones she heard about when she was sold over at Marlymont. Except over at Marlymont, they didn't just pray in those pits. They went there to learn letters, letters just like the ones she had seen on the gravestone where she had waited. They called those places for letter learning pit schools, but she only went once, because the pit school had been discovered. And that's when the troubles really began over at Marlymont.

Seems to have been fine when it was just black folks praying, but when they were actually learning, that was when all hell broke loose.

Afrika curled up in the shallow place she had scraped out and dragged some branches over her. She jammed her hand down into her pocket where she could feel the hush puppies. Weren't as good as a gun, these, but they were all she had.

The words, the melody, came like wisps of smoke through her dream.

> Steal away . . . steal away,
> Steal away to Jesus.
> Steal away, steal away home . . .
> I ain't got long to stay here.
> My Lord he calls to me.
> He calls me by the thunder,
> The trumpet sounds within my soul.
> I ain't got long to stay here.
> Steal away home.

Afrika whispered "no" in her sleep. "No, Mammee Bert," she was saying. "No . . . no. Don't go down there and get yourself whupped again. I know what it's like to get whupped, Mammee. I got a spiderweb on my back, yes I do."

It didn't make sense, she suddenly thought. She got that spiderweb after Talleystone, over at Marlymont. What was she doing back here hanging onto Mammee Bert's plum-black haunches?

"You're too big a girl to be in this bed with me. Only babies sleep in with Mammee Bert. Now you scoot."

"But Mammee Bert, you going to go to that

pit place and pray and they going to whup you."

"You worry 'bout yourself, gal. You just mind yourself. You get whupped, you ain't worth nothing."

Steal away . . . steal away . . . oh, she hated that song. In her sleep, she dreamed of pressing her hands to her ears, but the song still came, wheedling into her brain.

"They going to pull up your dress or make you go naked on the block," said the girl in the pen with her. "'Cause you ain't got no scars. Shows you a good girl. Don't get into no trouble. Me, I got bull-whip marks all over. Ain't going to pay nothing for me." The girl turned around and dropped her blouse. She had scars as bad as Mammee Bert's. "I ain't probably never going to git out of this pen," she said cheerfully. "But you be up there strutting away, and the price going to climb for you, gal."

"Frieda! Frieda! Show the bidders how you walk. That is a smooth stride. She can carry a lady's full-service silver tea tray — please note the strong shoulders — and she can set herself to splitting wood. This is just the gal you need indoors, out-

doors. She fit for anything, and she soon coming into her woman years."

The girl, Alma, had been right. One of the auctioneer's men had come to fetch her and strip off her clothes, and now she was on the block completely naked. Afrika couldn't believe they were talking about her. She had heard white people call her Frieda all her life. She was used to it. But now it was as if Frieda had become someone else. Walked right out of her body. There she was, standing in front of herself, watching herself being sold. The feeling had started back in the pens in the traders' yard when a man came up to both her and Alma, put on white gloves, and made them open their mouths. "Fine teeth, fine teeth," he said when he looked into Afrika's mouth. But then when Alma opened up, "This wench got cup worm in her teeth. She must be close to thirty years old, and them scars on her back. We gotta knock her price down. Four hundred most we can git for her."

They led them both off toward the block, and now this man was talking about her "woman years and her breeding time come up." She might as well be a sow. But if she couldn't be human and was just property, she would rather not be a living thing. So *while she stood naked she tried to think about what she might want to be. Once over at Talleystone when she had been up at the great house she had heard music floating out of the windows on the warm breeze. She peeked in and saw the beautiful wood thing the music came from. A woman was sitting on a bench pressing her fingers on something. Mammee Bert had told her it was a piano. That's what she wanted to be — a piano.*

"Do I hear one thousand? Do I hear one thousand?" The auctioneer's voice coiled through the warm air. "One thousand! Do I hear fifteen hundred?"

"Fifteen hundred." The auctioneer nodded toward a man at the corner of the block.

"Fifteen seventy-five. Do I hear fifteen seventy-five?" He looked around. "Sold! For fifteen hundred."

"What's your name?"

She couldn't speak to the man. It was as if she had already become a thing, like a piece of furniture. He asked her again. "She mute?" He turned to the auctioneer with a twist of panic in his voice.

"Naw, she can talk. Speak up, child, speak up. Don't you have anything to say to your new master?"

"I want to be a piano."

Afrika woke up with a start. The branches rustled with her sudden movement. She lay very quietly. She was sure she had not blurted out or screamed. But why had she awakened so suddenly? Then she smiled. She remembered Master Thomas's face when she had said she wanted to be a piano. He was stricken. He had just paid well over one thousand dollars for prize Negro flesh; a faultless, near-ripe young girl strong as anything, not a whip mark on her, and she just told him she wanted to be a piano. He'd bought himself a crazy gal!

Well, she couldn't sit around. It was getting dark, and she still had miles to go. She felt for the hush puppies, then sat up and cleared off the branches. She ate the last bit of cheese and some of the pork. She gave her calves a good rub to work out any kinks, and then she stopped for a full minute to listen carefully for any strange sounds in the night.

She was off. The moon was still down. Her legs felt better. She picked up her pace. Her eyes were so used to the night now, she felt part owl. She stretched out into the darkness and raced silently, streaking through woods like some earthly black comet.

Chapter 12

April 17, 1858

Boston, Massachusetts

Lucy heard the voices, the tinkle of laughter, drift out from the music room as she tried to read her book in a quiet corner of the walled garden. Daisy and Rose were entertaining Henry Van Schuyler and Edmund de Rosey yet again. How they tolerated them she would never know. She supposed Edmund de Rosey was not so bad. He, at least, had the sensitivity and intelligence to counterbalance some of Henry's worst aspects. But the problem was, no one else seemed to think Henry was all that bad.

Of course they hadn't overheard what Lucy had at the Adamses'. To Lucy it was all too clear what Henry was after — a rich bride. Thank heavens, she was too young to be in the running, and he was too fat to be of great appeal to any of her sisters. Her sisters, Daisy in particular, were most interested in Edmund. Edmund was fine, except Lucy judged him a bit dull, and all he seemed to talk about were subjects of recreation — fox hunting, duck hunting, a variety of card games with strange names. But he was beautifully mannered.

She was deep in her book and had not noticed the shadow slip across the sundial, but then she smelled the distinct odor of tobacco and coughed slightly.

"Oh, Miss Lucy!" Edmund de Rosey quickly ground out his cigar on the path. "Pardon me. I did not mean to interrupt your reading. I'm sorry. I hardly noticed you there under that screen of wisteria. I merely came out for a smoke."

"Oh, please, don't put it out on my account. A gentleman should be able to smoke outdoors whenever he pleases."

"That's very kind of you, but quite honestly I think there are many lovely flowers out here whose fragrance might be marred by the harsh odor of this." He looked with contempt at the slender cigar. Was he paying her a compliment?

Was he meaning that she was a flower? Lucy was so untutored in these things, she was not even sure. It seemed ironic — she being the only sister not named for a flower. And then, as if reading her mind, he said, "It is intriguing that you are called Lucy 'midst this sisterly bouquet."

And now Lucy did really blush.

"What's in a name? After all, a rose by any other name — even Lucy," he said, and she laughed, "would smell as sweet."

She could hardly believe it. This Southern gentleman was quoting Shakespeare to her! And here she thought he was only interested in hunting and cards!

"You know it, do you?" he asked.

"Of course. I read Shakespeare quite a bit with my grandfather."

"You are close to him?"

"Oh, yes. And you read Shakespeare, too, Mr. de Rosey?"

"A bit, but I'm no scholar . . ."

At that moment, Rose and Daisy came out into the garden with Henry Van Schuyler waddling between them. The two girls were convulsed with giggles over something Henry had just told them.

"So here you are, Cousin!" Henry said. "No doubt disturbing the serious pursuits of the studious Miss Lucy."

"We were discussing Shakespeare," Lucy replied tartly.

"Yes, I was about to tell Miss Lucy that with my languid nature, it was the only kind of mental activity that really engages me."

"Well, you're probably right about that."

"Come along, Edmund." Daisy tugged at his cuff. "We're going to take a walk over to the Somerset for tea."

"If it's not too far, I'll take it." Edmund laughed gently and slipped his arm through Daisy's.

Lucy could almost see the little shiver of excitement travel up Daisy's spine. She wondered what Daisy would have said had she known that he had quoted Shakespeare to her. How had he said it? "A rose by any other name — even Lucy."

She smiled. It was clever. It seemed somewhat out of tune with the lethargic nature Mr. de Rosey cultivated and advertised. He was perhaps quicker of wit than she had thought. Still, he was too languid for her, even if he did read poetry.

Chapter 13

April 17, 1858

At the end of Choptank River,

south of Camden, Delaware

The night welled up around her in all of its sweet, dark glory. Afrika loved the shadows, the purpling of the twilight sky, the promise of the blackness to come, and now, finally, it was here.

She had waited not just one night but four at the edge of the woods at the end of the Choptank for the moon to begin to wane, for the clouds. The nights had been brilliant, cloud-clear and star-bright. The North Star had burned with an intensity that bore right into her skull, into her brain, into her mind's eye. Blindfolded and turned around one hundred times she could find that old star, but there was no way she could cross this open field washed in moonlight. For too many miles she would be exposed.

She had passed through clearings before. Always, one had to count on coming upon a spot in the thick woods where there was a clearing, but never had there been one this broad. So she waited patiently with her dwindling food supplies, nursing her growing hunger for freedom. Now the right night had finally come, and oddly enough, Afrika was not ready. She clung to the darkness the way she had clung to Mammee Bert in the night. But she had to leave now. She could not wait another minute, not another second. The grass was tall, and if she had to, she would crawl on her belly and snake through it. That would be cover enough. On the far side of the field, Mrs. Page had said there were reports of haycocks, the bundled hay that stood in fields after it had been cut. So they, too, would offer her a hiding place.

For two hours she had made her way through the open field. Then suddenly the grass, which had been nearly waist high, vanished. In its place was the fresh, coarse stubble of a new-mown field. But as Mrs. Page had said, there were indeed some haycocks. Crawling on her belly, she made her way to the nearest one.

Maybe that was her first mistake, choosing the

nearest one, the most southerly one. Did she have just a sliver of a moment's hesitation? If she did, it was barely noticeable. Maybe just a quickening of the pulse before she burrowed into the stack of hay. But dawn would be coming soon, and it seemed so perfect. She would rest there until the next evening when she could set out on the highway to Camden. The old Negro lady's shack was right along the highway not more than three or four miles. The lady would tell her how to find the home of Ezekiel Hunn. She could be off with the first shadows of the evening and at the Hunn home before midnight.

She sank into a dreamless sleep. How long had she been asleep when she heard the footsteps? And did she actually smell them before she heard them? There was no time to even scream. She felt the hands grabbing her; a great gush of whisky breath washed over her face.

"We got one here, Jeptha! We got one!"

"Ya-hoo!"

The whoop peeled into the darkness. It was still night! And she could still see the North Star as they lifted her from the ground and into the wagon.

Chapter 14

April 17, 1858

Brookdale Farm,

summer home of Levi Bradford,

in Brookline, Massachusetts

The moon was like a silver mask. And the field was spread with bright webs of dew. Grandmother Pup used to call them fairies' linen, and when Pup had been alive, Lucy remembered summer nights at Brookdale when she and her grandmother would tiptoe across the lawn, through the fairies' linen, to look at the shooting stars. But now she was with Pap, and finally he was taking her owling.

She held his hand and tried not to shiver, for it was still cold, and her knit shawl was not quite warm enough. But she dared not admit it. He was taking her to the edge of the field, near a thin grove of trees. From there, an alley led into a deeper woods. He'd often seen great horned owls. Once he had seen a giant great gray and a barred owl, too. But it was the horned owl that he had seen most often, usually in the winter, on cold snowy nights. Only once before had he seen it on a spring night. Winter was the best time for owling. It would be very rare indeed to see one this time of year, but it was the great horned owl that Lucy wanted to see.

You had to be quiet, Pap told her, and not make any sudden movements and be ready to sit or stand still for a long time. Then, after a while, when everything felt right, Pap would make the call. He knew how to sing out *whoooo whooo* in just the right way, and if they were lucky and an owl was nearby, it might swoop down to the call.

They entered the grove now, and Pap touched her shoulder lightly and signaled her to stop. He lifted his hands to his mouth and tipped back his head. "*Whoooo whooo.*"

Lucy hoped the owl would come. The grove was so dark, and the shadows of the trees suddenly seemed ominous and frightening against the silvery moonlight. But she and Pap moved on, and with each step the forest grew more dense and still darker as the silver of the moonlight dissolved into the inky blackness of the woods. The dark shapes of fallen trees and stumps took on a life of their own.

"Think we'll see one?" Lucy asked, her voice tight.

"*Whoooo whooo,*" Pap called again. And then, suddenly, like a ribbon of sound, a soft *whoo whoo* came back.

Lucy squeezed her grandfather's hand harder and tried to keep her feet from dancing on the twigs and leaves.

Pap called back again. The owl's call was closer. Again Pap called.

This time he kneeled down and pointed toward an opening between the crowns of the trees. There was a stirring, then a shadow. Lucy could feel the wind on her face. It was an owl wind. Lucy touched her cheek where she had felt it.

A *whoo* came from the shadow. Pap slipped the cover from the lantern he had carried and raised it in the night.

On a limb of a nearby tree perched an immense owl. Its eyes were bigger than Lucy had imagined. Its horned tufts poked the night. Its legs were fat with fluffy down that sheathed them like two velvety muffs. The ruff on its neck puffed.

The owl looked directly at Lucy with huge yellow eyes set in disks of flat brown feathers. Lucy felt herself hypnotized. It bobbed its head, pumped its wings — once, twice — then lunged from the branch, lifting effortlessly in silent flight onto the soft edges of the silvery night. It became a shadow gliding across the moon.

In the carriage back to Boston, Lucy tried to remember the soft silence of the owl. She looked out the window of the carriage. The darkness still scared her. Bare, tangled branches could become witches' fingers; tree stumps could become dancing goblins. But when she thought of the deep silence of the owl in flight, she longed for that woods. She wondered if she might ever grow used to it and find in the darkness a calm, in the night a refuge, and even an unspoken meaning.

Lucy woke late the next morning at her grandfather's. She went downstairs to the kitchen, and Zephy was just taking some muffins from the oven.

"Has Pap already eaten?"

"Oh, yes, Lucy, he's been up for hours."

"I went owling last night."

"I know it." Zephy smiled.

"Is Pap in the library?"

"Yes."

"Well, I think I'll take a muffin and some chocolate in there and . . ."

"Oh, no! No!" Zephy set the muffin tin down with a loud clatter on the soapstone counter. "He's not to be disturbed."

"What do you mean?" Lucy was perplexed. "Is he . . . is he examining someone, here at home?"

"No . . . no," Zephy stammered. "No . . . he only . . ."

"Well, what in the world is it, Zephy?"

At that moment, the doorbell rang. Zephy inhaled sharply. Wringing her hands, she bustled out of the kitchen.

Still in her stocking feet, Lucy padded into the back pantry hall between the kitchen and the dining room. It had one door, thankfully ajar, through which she could peek into the entry hall. A gentleman with a dilapidated beaver hat stood in the hall.

"Austin Bearse with some tickets for Doctor Bradford."

"Yes, sir." Zephy curtsied deeply.

"Would it be possible for me to see the doctor now? Is he in?"

"Yes, sir. Please follow me." Zephy's voice, though hardly above a whisper, was full of deference.

Lucy's mouth hung open in disbelief. How did this weather-beaten old man get led directly into her grandfather, where she, his own flesh and blood, was not permitted into the library? She who always ate her muffin at Pap's desk or, if he was working, by the fireplace whenever she spent the night. She was furious. Absolutely furious. She had always counted on Pap, even more so during all this wedding nonsense. If he began to ignore her now . . . oh, she could not finish the thought.

She went back upstairs to the bedroom to finish dressing and began by brushing her hair vigorously. The next thing you'd know, he'd be canceling their owling date for tomorrow night. She put down her brush and looked at herself in the mirror. Her eyes were smoky dark, and the red blotches on her cheeks were spreading like miniature wildfires. She took a deep breath. *Think! Think, Lucy. Be calm and think. Don't let your emotions get the best of you. This is not at all like Pap. Something is going on. In order to find out, you'll have to be smart.*

Putting on her dress but not her shoes, Lucy crept down the great winding staircase that led from the upper floors to the entrance hall. There was a landing with a niche, which made a very nice seat and from the entrance hall was totally invisible.

Lucy did not have to wait long. She heard the creak of the heavy oak doors to the library. Then her grandfather's voice.

"Yes, yes, and you think Bowditch can handle it with his carryall."

There was a muffled reply that Lucy could not make out. "So, Lev, the tickets are for tonight at Meionaon, half past seven. Come in through the office entrance on School Street."

Tonight, Meionaon, half past seven!

Chapter 15

April 18, 1858

136 Beacon Street,

Boston, Massachusetts

Not you, too!" Delphinia sighed as Lucy walked into the music room.

Despite his fat fingers, Henry Van Schuyler was doing a remarkably good job with a Mozart sonata as Rose looked over his shoulder.

"What do you mean, not me, too?"

The music stopped, and Henry and Rose looked up.

"That scowl," Delphy exclaimed. "Between you and Daisy, this is the grimmest house on Beacon Street. I expected you to come in utterly jubilant from your owling expedition. What, no owls?"

"No, no, it's nothing. What's wrong with Daisy?"

"Oh, Edmund de Rosey sent a note over this

morning saying that he cannot attend the Belk-naps' daffodil dance for Iris."

"He did!" Henry Van Schuyler looked mildly surprised.

"Oh my goodness," Lucy moaned. "I completely forgot. Do I have to go to that?"

"I'm sure you could beg off." And then he lowered his voice. "I doubt if Robert Shaw will be there, as it is examination time at Harvard."

"Well, ladies, I must be going." Henry heaved his bulk from the spindly piano stool. "I shall see you tonight, Rose, at the daffodil dance, I trust." He made a stiff little bow to all three girls and left the room.

Lucy sank into the nearest armchair. "I cannot abide him!" she muttered as soon as she heard the maid shut the front hall door.

"He's not that bad," Rose said.

"You aren't falling for him, Rose? You can't be."

"Of course not."

"He's so crude. I can't believe he's a relative of Elwyn's," Lucy said.

"As I understand it, Henry was orphaned and did not have Elwyn's advantages."

"He certainly did not lack for food!" At this they all laughed.

"He's a great gossip," Rose interjected, "but it is harmless gossip. He seems to know everything and everybody about town, even though he is a New Yorker."

"And he doesn't take himself too seriously." Delphy paused and then said emphatically, "I like that."

Lucy wondered about what her sisters had just said. They seemed to like Henry Van Schuyler for all the reasons she did not. It was as if he functioned as some sort of drawing room pet for them — and a singularly unattractive one at that: obese, of lurid coloration, and swirling in the perfumed eddies of hair pomade.

Lucy retreated to her bedroom until Miss Leverett, her French and drawing teacher, came for afternoon lessons. Pap had never even come out of his study to say good-bye. She knew he was a busy man, but still. . . . She felt totally glum.

Lucy was just finishing her French lesson with Miss Leverett when there was a knock on the parlor door.

"Come in," Miss Leverett called.

Bridget, the upstairs maid, stood in the doorway. She was holding a cream-colored envelope. "A message for Miss Lucy, from her grandfather."

"Oh!" Lucy sprang up, smiling. She took the envelope, tore it open, and began reading her grandfather's spidery script.

Dear Child,

How lucky we were to see the great horned owl last night. It must have come out just for you. I fear I must cancel our expedition for tomorrow evening as I have some unexpected business that must be attended to immediately. I promise that we shall go again soon.

Most affectionately,

Pap

P.S. Have a grand time at the daffodil dance. I am sure you shall be the loveliest flower of them all — despite your name!

"Lucy, is something wrong?" Miss Leverett asked.

Everything! Lucy thought. *And he's trying to buy me off with silly compliments. Well, bird droppings on that!* She looked up. If she were going to do what she was planning to do, she had better get smarter about it — or at least conceal her emotions better. She swallowed. "Oh, it really is nothing, Miss Leverett. May I try the verbs one more time? It's the subjunctive tense that troubles me."

"Why yes of course, dear."

Lucy was her old self again. Normal, attentive, industrious.

"*Chante, chantes, chante.* I would sing, you would sing, he would sing. . . ."

If he had simply banished her from the study and Mr. Bearse had not shown up, and if he had not canceled the owling expedition, Lucy would never have thought of going to Meionaon Hall. It had been easy begging off the daffodil dance. Bridget and Mary, the maids, were the only ones home that evening as it was Cook's night off. So it was easy for Lucy to slip out of the house at 136 Beacon just before seven.

She walked straight up Beacon to the corner of Charles and crossed to the Common. Before she left, she had grabbed a worn cloak from the scullery closet, and a bonnet and basket. Now she looked like any of the numerous serving girls who worked in the grand houses on Beacon, hurrying for the day-off visit to her family in south Boston.

The Tremont Temple was on the corner of School and Bromfield streets. But she had clearly heard Mr. Bearse say that the meeting was in Meionaon Hall, and her grandfather should pass in through the office entrance on School Street.

Lucy rounded the corner. Not more than fifty feet down the narrow street, a cluster of stovepipe-hatted men were going into a narrow doorway. She pressed herself as close to the buildings as possible and made her way down the darkening street.

At a quarter past the hour, she glanced over her shoulder and saw more stovepipe-hatted men behind her.

Lucy ducked into a doorway, under a sign that read FEMALE ACCOUNTANTS. From there she could see but not be seen.

She thought of the great horned owl of the night before, gliding silently on its wings of hollow bone and velvet down. How odd that a creature in one sense so fragile, could possess such power. But, in fact, it was the very delicacy of the bird's construction that enabled it to kill so effectively and with consummate stealth. One did not have to be all muscle and brawn to vanquish.

Suddenly she caught sight of her grandfather's figure in the double-tiered cloak. And at that moment she also saw Austin Bearse step from the temple's side door and motion the cluster of gentlemen in.

Several of them she recognized. There was the Reverend Theodore Parker and Wendell Phillips, and Richard Dana.

A glimmer, just a small memory like the lambent glow of an ember, began to flicker in Lucy's brain. It had happened many years ago. How long ago? Six, seven years ago. She would have been just seven or eight herself. But there was that terrible time.

She had been sitting with Pup looking at a book of Aesop's fables. Pap had roared into Pup's sitting room and actually shouted something. What was it? What had it been? He had sunk down into his chair and buried his face in his hands. Then Pup got up and went to him and said, "Sims, he lost?" And Pap's shoulders just shook. His voice quaking, he said, "My dear, Massachusetts has sent its first fugitive slave back into slavery!" Lucy had never seen him cry before, nor after, not even when Pup died.

Politics was usually banned from the dinner-table conversation, but it wasn't after this. There were long weeks when Lucy's father and mother argued about this Sims case. And afterward they never spoke of these matters; Lucy sensed that an understanding had been reached, that these terrible things would never again be discussed within the family because there was too much disagreement.

She leaned farther out of the shadows. More men streamed in. Lucy's eyes widened. The knowledge suddenly struck her. This was what her mother had called "the fool Vigilance Committee."

Stunned, she retreated back into the doorway. She had always known that her grandfather was against slavery. But was he actually an abolitionist, like Mr. Garrison and Mr. Phillips? You could be against slavery but not quite be an abolitionist, Lucy thought. An abolitionist was a person like Mr. Phillips with his wild hair and inflamed speech or like Mr. Garrison, gaunt and eyes burning like a biblical prophet, proclaiming the Word in his newspaper *The Liberator*. To be an abolitionist was like being a warrior. Her grandfather was a doctor and a scholar. Was he a warrior, too?

She knew he hated slavery, hated the fugitive slave law, but was he in fact a warrior against it? Would he break the law of the land himself and help slaves or help others to help fugitive slaves? There were fines, there was prison, you could be arrested!

Her ancestors had written the laws of the Commonwealth — would they dare break them?

Suddenly her whole world was turning upside down. There was so much to think about. Lucy pulled her cloak tighter and crossed the street. She did not want to return home immediately, so instead she turned down Washington Street past the Boston Theater, whose billboards advertised a list of vaudeville acts: The Fantastic Parrot Lady, Mitchell the Magnificent, Goldie and the Prairie Flowers. She was in a section of town where she would never be allowed to go unescorted, or even escorted, for that matter. But she didn't care.

Lucy turned down a small street, a service road for busy Washington Street. Between signs for livery stables and establishments for quartering horses, she spotted the backstage entrance to the

Boston Theater. Despite the coolness of the evening, people were sitting out on its stairways and fire escapes, people whose lives were as different as humanly possible from her own. She paused and pressed herself into the shadows, just to watch for a minute or two.

She blinked as she saw a familiar figure dash up the side stairs. Her first instinct was to call out to Edmund de Rosey, but then she recalled that neither she nor de Rosey had a very good explanation for being there.

Before he reached the top, the door opened, and a woman came out. Her red hair frizzed like a great cloud over her head.

"Eddie!" she squealed, but her small mouth seemed hard and mirthless.

"Goldie!"

So this was one of the Prairie Flowers!

Lucy crouched behind some slop barrels and watched. The woman was scandalously dressed in a turquoise gown. Lucy could not believe it. She never knew breasts grew that big!

The woman and Edmund were embracing. Lucy watched, transfixed. Then she shut her eyes tight. She would not watch, but she was too scared to move. And to think that she had been wondering what Daisy would feel if she had known Edmund had quoted Shakespeare to her! What would Daisy say at the sight of this? Oh, poor Daisy!

Lucy was unsure how she got from behind the barrels and out of Mason Street. But when she arrived at her grandfather's house on Beacon, she had composed herself. Her first order of business was to convince Zephy to let her stay the night and wait for Pap in his study.

"It's all right if I go in there now, isn't it, Zephy?" she said sweetly.

"But does your family know you're here?"

Lucy hadn't thought about that. "Well, I forgot to tell Bridget or Mary. Do you suppose Jeremy could just dash up the street and tell them where I am?"

Zephyra looked at Lucy narrowly. "All right," she finally said. "You go on into your Pap's library. I don't know what time he'll be back. It might be late. You want some hot chocolate?"

"No, thank you."

Lucy went into the study. She'd wait up all night if she had to. Yes, she would.

* * *

She had dozed off with her head on the desk, but as soon as she heard the tap of the cane in the foyer she jerked awake. A column of butterflies rose in her diaphragm as the doors to the study opened, and her grandfather entered.

She looked straight at him. "I want to know what's going on, Pap. I'm sick and tired of being left out of things. I want things to make sense."

Lucy's grandfather eased himself into the chair by the fireplace, but the fire had long ago gone cold.

"So you want things to make sense."

"Yes." The word was no more than a whisper.

Lucy got up from behind the desk. She came and sat down on the floor beside him and put her hands on his knees. "Pap, I have got to know. I know that you are against slavery. I know you hate the fugitive slave law. But Pap, are you an abolitionist? Would you really break the law?"

"I am breaking the law, dear child. I am breaking this law every and any chance I get."

Chapter 16
April 18, 1858

On the road to Camden, Delaware

They had bound her feet and her hands, and they had thrown Afrika in the back of the wagon.

It had all happened so quickly that the full enormity had not quite hit her. But now it did. After weeks of running, after all the help from people like Mr. and Mrs. Page and Captain Briggs, it had all come down to this, being caught by two liquored-up slave hunters. They didn't even have dogs. They just snatched her out of that haycock.

"How's he doin', Jeptha?" the driver asked.

"Doan know. Lemme check." The one called Jeptha turned around and poked her with the butt end of his rifle. "How you doin', boy?"

Boy! They were so stupid they thought she was

a boy, even though her hat had fallen off and one of her braids had come down. She grunted in reply.

He gave her a sharper poke with the rifle. "You talk to me right snappy, you hear? We going to make a lot of money off you, and we don't want you looking and acting bad like some worthless piece of horse manure." They both laughed at this. "So how you doin'?"

"Fine," she muttered.

"That's more like it, boy."

What did it mean, that they thought she was a boy?It might mean they were drunker than Afrika first thought, and if they were drunker than she thought. . . . An idea niggled in the back of her mind. Maybe, just maybe, she could fool them again, fool them somehow and get away. She wouldn't have much time.

She had to think hard and think fast. She tried wiggling her hands. They had bound them tight, but not impossibly tight. Suppose she could get them loose, where would she run?

They had a rifle. They could shoot her. Well, how straight could they shoot if they were this drunk? That was some comfort. She would try working on the knots.

After several minutes, she realized the knots were too tight. It was probably impossible to get them loose.

Afrika despaired. Her face was shoved against some sort of pack, and she could smell moldy bread and strong cheese. She was terribly hungry, and it smelled good to her, even the moldy bread. Her hush puppies still smelled good, too. They were laced with lots of honey to attract the dogs. Suddenly she had a thought.

She'd kept the hush puppies in a canvas bag tucked inside the front of her shirt. She could still feel them pressing against her chest. Her elbows weren't tied. She might be able to work her arms and get the hush puppies to drop out. She squirmed around a bit.

In less than two minutes, the cloth bag had been worked out from under her shirt and was on the wagon floor. Her wrists were tied, but she had some finger movement, and between her fingers and her teeth she was able to open the bag.

It took her five tries before she got the first hush

puppy into the men's pack, for she certainly did not want to pick up the poisonous thing with her teeth. She dropped it in beside the bread and the moldy cheese. She soon had the knack and dropped the others in. Now she supposed she had to wait until they got hungry. But when would that be? She waited about one minute.

"You got any food, mister? I'm hungry."

"Shut up."

"If'n you going to make a lot of money off me, they don't want some half-starved, skinny colored boy. I like to have fits when I don't eat."

"He got a point, Luke."

"I don't know. That lady packed up some stuff for us yesterday, but I think the bread gone moldy."

"Good enough for a darkie. Jest give him some of that."

"I don't give no mind to moldy bread," Afrika said, careful to keep her voice low.

"All right." The one called Jeptha turned around in the seat to reach for the satchel with the food, but in his state of inebriation it proved difficult. "Hey, stop the wagon, Luke, I can't get at the food."

"All right. I could use something myself."

The wagon stopped. Jeptha reached for the food bag. "Hey, what's this? That old lady must of put in some pone fingers. My, how I like those."

"Gimme one, too."

"There are only two I can see."

"Well, he done say he like moldy bread." They both laughed heartily at this.

"Here's your moldy bread," Jeptha said and tossed it to Afrika.

Afrika saw a way now. In fact, she was just about to say she couldn't eat it with her hands tied when she saw that both slave hunters were biting into the hush puppies at the same time. She kept her head down but watched them from the corners of her eyes. They bit, they swallowed. They bit again. She sat perfectly still.

"Ummmmm." The sound came from Luke. "Sweet with hon — " There was a terrible gagging sound, then a gasping. "Jep — " The sound stuck in his throat like a piece of broken glass.

Afrika heard more coughing. She looked up. A contorted face leaned over her. Luke's hand grabbed her by the throat. She felt it tighten around her windpipe, but then it relaxed and let go.

He fell sideways, with a sharp crack as his head hit the wheel of the wagon. Jeptha slumped forward, gasped twice, and then there was utter silence.

Chapter 17

April 18, 1858
154 Beacon Street,

Boston, Massachusetts

First, Lucy, there was the Shadrach case, but thank God he got away. Then hardly had Shadrach escaped the slave hounds when they got Thomas Sims, April 3, 1851. He was the first slave, after the fugitive slave law had been passed, to be sent back into slavery by Massachusetts since the Revolution. Three years later it was Anthony Burns.

"It was our own courts, right here in Boston, that handed down the decisions to send these men back into slavery. They actually had to put chains around the courthouse, so angry were the citizens of Boston. Imagine a seat of law and order becoming a chained slave fortress.

"I said then, and I will say it again now, that courts obliged to sit protected by bayonets will not long sit in the Commonwealth of Massachusetts."

Levi Bradford paused for a moment, and then he continued. "But it was true, and it is still true. You cannot have law in a community if it can only be obeyed at the point of a bayonet. Since the days of Sims and Burns, that has been the case.

"Daniel Webster, my old friend, has supported the fugitive slave law, and the proclamation issued by President Fillmore after the escape of Shadrach, directing the prosecution of all those who abetted the escape of a slave. To this day, I shall never understand him. U.S. Commissioner Edward G. Loring, a man I have known since boyhood, sent Anthony Burns back to his owners in the South.

"But it was not only men of the law who supported this outrage. It was gentlemen of commerce as well, the men of Milk Street and State Street whose family businesses profit from a slave-based economy, who cheered when Burns and Sims were returned."

"Did Papa cheer?" Lucy asked, thinking of her father's office on Milk Street, from which he ran the family's shipping and mill businesses.

Levi Bradford sighed deeply. "It was a very difficult time in our family. There were differences of opinion over the issues of abolition and how far one should go in terms of civil disobedience. We don't discuss it anymore. No, your father did not cheer. But I would be lying if I were to say that he was not relieved when the fates of Mr. Sims and Mr. Burns were sealed. It made his life at home with your mother much easier."

"But not for you?"

"No, how could it ever? These are the hours of our disgrace. Our own government officials have become hostile to the founding principles, principles that many of us hold most dear. So along with nearly two hundred others who compose the Vigilance Committee, yes, we break the law.

"I, myself, am on the finance committee with Henry Bowditch — you remember him, dear, he always brings you maple candy for Christmas — and a few others. We raise money to help finance the fugitives' escape. In so doing, I break the law — I am an outlaw in my own dear Commonwealth. A pirate, I suppose, declaring his own law on a chartless sea."

"Is it just money-raising? Do you do anything else?"

"Mostly, it is money. Yes, ninety-nine percent of the time it is raising money, writing checks, making sure the money gets where it needs to go."

"But one percent of the time?" Lucy asked.

"Yes, well, Lucy, one percent of the time I am called upon to perform a special service. You have heard perhaps of something called the Underground Railroad?"

"Pap, yes! Is it real? It sounds so . . . so unbelievable. Is it like train cars that run underground? How does it work? It sounds so fantastical."

"It is fantastical. No doubt about it. But it is very real. And it runs through Boston. Not cars, mind you. But it has stops, called stations, and conductors who lead the people to the next safe place on their long journey to Canada, where they can live free."

"What do you do, Pap?"

"Well, I help them if they arrive sick because I am a doctor, and . . . and . . ." He hesitated. "I am sometimes what they call a conductor."

"A conductor!" Such an ordinary, plain word, but it suddenly blossomed in Lucy's mind.

"Yes. I take newly arrived fugitives. Often we refer to them as parcels, or some inanimate object — "

"Like dates from the Levant!" Lucy blurted out.

Levi Bradford looked aghast.

"When they told you that the dates had arrived in time for dessert at the Adamses', that's when you had to leave, wasn't it? You didn't have gout at all. I saw you, Pap, practically running down Mount Vernon."

Levi cleared his throat. "As I was saying, on certain rare occasions, I take these parcels and conduct them, as it were, to the stations farther west and north of here. Drive them myself in the hansom, the one I use for house calls."

"And owling." Lucy blinked and smiled. "That's it, isn't it, Pap? Owling is just an excuse so you can go out at night."

"Now, how the devil did you figure that out?"

"Pap, you have always had a passion for a very limited range of raptors — red-tailed hawks, eagles, peregrine falcons. Suddenly, after all these years, you are interested in owls."

"I hope it isn't that transparent to the rest of the world."

"No, no. Don't worry. Nobody knows you the way I do, Pap. So is owling still canceled for tomorrow night?"

"In other words, you want to go — is that what you're asking?"

"Yes."

Chapter 18
April 19, 1858
Boston, Massachusetts

Summer complaint, my foot!" The voice was full of mirth. Lucy had gone round through the back garden, when she had returned from her grandfather's. She was picking a bouquet of the miniature daffodils that grew outside the scullery door, which was open. The words stopped her.

The maids were just inside, but this was neither Mary nor Bridget. It had to be Dulcey from down the street, and she had to be talking about Edmund de Rosey. Had she seen him, too, last night? It was very possible. Serving girls often went to Washington Street to catch the plays and new vaudeville acts passing through Boston.

"So was that his excuse?"

"Yes, but Dulcey, how can you stand him? I mean, he's so fat." That was Mary's voice.

"And so pinky, like a pig . . . swine pink. That's what Miss Lucy says. You should hear her on the subject of Mr. Van Schuyler."

It was not Edmund de Rosey they were talking about at all, but Henry Van Schuyler. He, too, seemed to have missed the daffodil dance and had been paying court to Dulcey, the Randall Philipotses' upstairs maid who lived three doors down.

"So where'd he take you? Tea dancing at the Somerset?"

"No, he came round rather late. We went down to the Jellicoe Gardens for a late supper."

"Why'd he come for you so late? I mean, if it wasn't summer complaint, and he was getting out of the daffodil dance . . ."

"How should I know? He's a very busy man. Works in a great financial house in New York, something to do with the stock exchange. He comes up here a lot now 'cause of his cousin Elwyn Van Schuyler with all them engagement parties for Miss Iris."

As the conversation drew to a close, Lucy quickly retreated back into the garden and set down her bouquet. Dropping to her knees, she began prodding at the earth, as if setting out some seeds. She had much to think about.

Both Edmund de Rosey and Henry Van Schuyler had dodged out of the daffodil dance to be with women who were beneath their station. Odd behavior for two men who seemed to enjoy the material pleasures of life. Both needed a young bride with a healthy dowry. And Henry was not only indiscreet but just plain stupid to be taking up with a household servant. The news would be up and down Beacon Street in no time.

It was one thing to go off into the murky netherworld of Boston and meet with an actress on the side stairs of a vaudeville theater, but consorting with a house servant was positively harebrained. House servants were notorious gossips. Well, no one had accused Henry of having an abundance of intelligence. Even Elwyn had said that Henry had been slow in school, but to his family's amazement he was "working out quite well" at the brokerage house. Well, this thing with Dulcey would set him back if he pursued it in earnest.

"Ah, Miss Lucy. Gardening, are you?" Dulcey called out from the scullery.

"Just weeding." Lucy clawed at some violets. "Violets can be quite invasive and not leave any room for the annuals Mama likes to plant."

"Oh, you don't say." Dulcey spoke absently, as if her mind was far away. Probably not that distant. Probably just as far as last night at Jellicoe Gardens.

What some girls would settle for when it came to a man's attention.

Chapter 19

April 18, 1858

The home of Ezekiel Hunn outside

Camden, Delaware

Afrika's face was smeared with blood. "I am a friend. My name is Joe Bell," she said, and then she collapsed in the doorway.

"Ezekiel!" she heard the woman scream as she fell.

Afrika was soon revived, however. The bleeding came from superficial wounds caused by the ropes binding her wrists. In trying to loosen them with her teeth, she had cut her mouth. Although the cut was not deep, it had bled heavily.

The Hunns were greatly relieved to see that Afrika was in much better condition than she appeared at first. But she was enormously agitated and could hardly get her story out fast enough.

"You have to run out there on Camden Road,

two dead men. Slave catchers. . . . I killed them. Hush puppies. . . . Captain Briggs. . . ."

The story came out in bits, but finally they realized the urgency of what she was saying. Afrika had killed two slave hunters, and there was a three-mile trail of blood, her blood, right to their front door.

"Eliza," Ezekiel said suddenly. "I'm going to haul the sow up to David Appley's and have him slaughter it for me and butcher it as he always does."

"What idea is this? Thee never slaughters so early."

"I'll think of some excuse. But David will help me. We shall drive back over the route this child followed from the field — dripping that sow's blood the whole way."

"And what about the two dead men? Where will thee hide their bodies? They'll hardly pass for piglets!"

"'Tis not a bad idea, Eliza. Under the sow."

Four hours later, four men rode up to Ezekiel Hunn's house. Thick clouds of smoke rose from just beyond his barnyard.

"Did you see two men around these parts?"

"Ah, would they be from the wagon up the road a piece?" Ezekiel said, cool as could be.

"Yes, those be the men."

"I passed that way with my butchered sow. I saw the wagon, but no sign of the men." That should explain the trail of blood.

Two days later, Afrika was on her way again. David Appley had come for his share of pork, driving his buckboard straight into the Hunns' large, cold house. The Hunns, who were known for their curing of ham and salt beef, had kept immense slabs of bacon wrapped in cloth, hams, and some sides of beef for him from the last slaughtering.

When he came out, no one noticed that the meat rode perhaps a foot higher than usual in the cart. Underneath was Afrika. The two headed back in the direction of the Appleys' farm, which was far off the main road and as yet not an object of suspicion to the authorities. By nightfall, Appley and Afrika set out in their true direction, north toward Middletown.

Afrika no longer lay beneath the slabs of meat, which might have offered more protection from the steady drizzle. But she didn't mind. She rode in the back of the cart. Mrs. Appley, who was lame with a crooked back and seemed not much bigger than a child, rode on the buckboard seat next to her husband. Afrika held her crutches in the back. She was no longer Joe Bell. She was Susie, Mrs. Appley's sister's serving girl, free serving girl. And that was just what David and Jessamine Appley were arguing about right now.

"They'll be able to tell in a minute, David, that these manumission papers don't amount to anything. It's the worst-looking forgery job I've ever seen."

"Now, how many have you seen, Jess?" David Appley asked good-naturedly. "You a counterfeiter? Writing bad bank drafts?"

"Don't fool with me, David." For a little crippled woman, Afrika thought, she sure could give lip. "I think it's better that we say she's a slave girl belonging to my sister."

"But Ezekiel said they're looking for a slave girl disguised as a boy. It's too risky."

"No, it's not. We got a slave girl not disguised as a boy. We got a plain girl here." She paused and turned around. "Aren't you?" And as she said the words, another thought came to her. "Stop the wagon!"

"What now? Good Lord, Jessamine."

"Don't use the Lord's name in vain, David."

David sighed as he watched his wife hold out the papers in the rain.

"What in the name . . ." He paused. His small wife shot him a venomous look. He began again. "What in the name of a gopher's toes are you doing?"

Jessamine swallowed a chuckle. "I'm wetting these down so they'll look all smudgy and terrible, and folks won't know the difference between this and a bad forgery — which, of course, is what these are." Then she flung them down on the ground.

"What?" David Appley gasped.

"A little mud never hurt anything. It might help in a case like this."

"Jessamine, I do declare." He got down off the wagon and retrieved the papers, which were now stained and so soggy as to be almost unreadable.

They were never read. The trip to John Hunn's was uneventful. It passed quickly for Afrika as she listened to the gentle bickering between the two Appleys. They let her off just outside of Smyrna. She had specific instructions on how to identify and approach John Hunn's house, where she arrived at dawn.

John Hunn was every bit as nice as his brother Ezekiel, but he seemed extremely nervous to Afrika.

After she had finished the last bit of oatmeal, John Hunn jumped from his seat. He paced the floor.

"Afrika. . . ." He cleared his throat and began again. "I don't mean to scare thee, child, but there has been a very unsettling turn of events in the last week in this region. I had not been fully aware of the gravity of the situation until just last evening before you arrived."

"Yes, sir," she answered hesitantly. After what she had already been through in the last few days, she could not imagine much worse. Only. . . . The thought struck her like a piece of cold metal on a winter morning. Her whole being seemed to chill. What if this man didn't want to help her?

From his coat pocket, John Hunn suddenly

yanked out a handbill. On it were two pictures. Afrika did not know what the letters said, but one image she did know. There she was, badly drawn, nose too narrow, brow too low, eyes hooded in a strange way. But it was her. She ran her tongue over the gap between her teeth. It didn't really matter about the nice little bone piece Mr. Page had given her.

"This is not good." John Hunn spoke softly. "It doesn't matter that the picture barely resembles thee. In the last few weeks the bridge over to Wilmington has been nearly impossible. With this picture out, any female of roughly thy size and age will never get across."

Afrika buried her face in her hands.

"It is simply too dangerous, child." Was he saying that there was no way? That he could do nothing? Was she to turn back now?

A shudder passed through Afrika's body. She could not form the words to ask the questions. She felt a hand on her shoulder.

"I can take thee as far as New Castle, and there is supposed to be a schooner coming in within the next two to three days, bound for Philadelphia. This is the only chance. And even then, I don't know how thee shall not be noticed in New Castle or where thee can hide. We have no safe houses there."

Afrika looked at him and thought a moment. He was a nice man and a good man, but he was scared, and what did white folks know about being scared? Just like Captain Briggs nearly got sick when he saw the scars on her back. She had not come this far to be dragged down by other folks' fears. "I don't need no safe house. I be sleeping in the woods all these weeks. I jumped in a river back there and didn't know how to swim. I'll find me a place to be. You leave that to me."

John Hunn sighed. "If this handbill hadn't come out."

"What does it say?"

He began reading. "Two-hundred-dollar reward. Ran away from Jenk Thomas on Sunday night the twenty-sixth of December. Negro girl Frieda, stands just over five feet, slender build, with a gap between front teeth. She escaped from the Marlymont Plantation near Summer Springs, Virginia, along with eight other Negroes in the accompaniment of Harriet Tubman but is thought to have become separated from the group and to still be at large, perhaps disguised as a boy. I will pay two hundred dollars for the apprehension and delivery of the girl or to have her confined so I can get her. Jenk Thomas, Marlymont Plantation, the second of April, 1858."

John Hunn's hands had trembled as he read the handbill. Now he folded it and pursed his lips as he stared at the floor.

"Tell me something," Afrika said suddenly.

"What's that, child?"

"Could you buy a piano for two hundred dollars?"

He looked taken aback by the question. "More than one, I think."

"You don't say." *Well, I ain't no piano,* Afrika thought. She jammed the piece of bone into the gap between her teeth. "You got that food ready, Mr. Hunn?"

"Yes, Afrika."

She barely waited until the dusk had settled on the land when she was out their door, moving so swiftly, so silently, that she was swallowed into the night.

The food had run out after two days. Luckily the slop barrel was near the back end of the hotel's porch. So between the scraps of old bread, half-eaten vegetables, and meat bones, hunger was not a problem.

As soon as Afrika had seen the big old sprawling white hotel with the deep porch, she had known she had a place to hide. Long before Talleystone or Marlymont, when she had been little, before they had taken her from her mother, she had played with other little slave children under the big porch of the great house. She had loved the shadowy coolness, the sharp reeds of sunlight that fell between the cracks. You had to be quiet under a porch and leave behind your songs and even your whispers. It was where the cats came to have their kittens. And sometimes you found great treasures. A lady's earring, a little girl's hair-bow.

She was fine under this big old porch in New Castle. The real problem was that there had been no sign of any schooner. At night she could slip out from under the porch and go down to the docks, but there were no large boats. New Castle was a shabby little harbor with nothing bigger than a skipjack in it.

One morning, an hour or more before dawn, she heard the cook's voice, crankier than ever, in the yard scolding her young nephew.

"Peter, that is the last time I set you to feed the chickens. By gum, if your head warn't screwed on you'd forget it. How you could leave that gate open, I'll never know. Them chickens's probably under the porch. Now you crawl under there and get them."

Afrika's breath froze in her throat. Sure enough, there were two chickens not six feet away from where she'd been sleeping. And then she felt the boy's footsteps. She heard movement near the lat-ticework that formed the wall between the porch floor and the ground. There was a hole torn in one part through which she had entered, as had the chickens, and now the boy.

"*Chirrrhk . . . chirrhk.*" The boy made the soft, feathery sound in the back of his throat as he crawled on all fours through the hole.

Suddenly a sound tore through the dark close air, a terribly low snarling growl full of fury. Then there was a scuttling noise as the boy backed out so fast he nearly took part of the latticework with him.

"Auntie, there's a mad dog in there. I ain't going."

There was no need. The growl that had torn from Afrika's throat had scared out the chickens as well as the boy. But now Afrika knew she was going to have to get out herself. The cook wouldn't tolerate a mad dog so close to her chicken house. It wouldn't be long before she or someone else would be out with a shotgun.

Afrika was trying to sort out her thoughts. There was still a large commotion in the yard as the cook and her nephew chased the two chickens back to their pen. Suddenly Afrika heard a sizzling "*pssst.*" The sound zipped low through the air from the other side of the porch.

"*Psst* — Afrika! It's me, John Hunn."

Afrika could hardly believe it. How had he found her? She opened her eyes wider in the dim light. There he was, peering through the lattice at the end of the porch. She crawled over as quickly as she could and pressed her face so close to the lattice she could feel his warm breath on her cheeks.

"What are you doing here?"

"The question is why I didn't think of this porch to begin with as a hiding place for thee. But never mind that. There's no ship coming. I thought thee would wait an extra day or so. Thee must leave now before dawn. Thee has another hour before full light. I cannot take thee. I will decoy them, lead them on a goose chase. Thee must go on this road five miles. But there is less than an hour to spare. Can thee run five miles in that time, keeping low?"

"Yes, sir."

"There is a washout down the road from spring rains between here and the Wilmington bridge. Creek flooded and all. A funeral procession will be coming. There will be a breakdown in the wagon hauling the coffin. They will have to unload the casket to fix the axle. Take it to the side of the road by a big hickory nut tree. Thee must be there in the tall grass by the hickory nut."

"Yes, sir."

And once again John Hunn watched as Afrika seemed to melt into thin air.

Chapter 21

April 28, 1858

Crossing the bridge

at Wilmington, Delaware

Total darkness. It didn't matter that they had drilled air holes. There was simply no light. And the dead man she lay on was skinny and bony, and there wasn't any chance that he was going to fatten up. He wore a stick pin in his cravat and the head of it was digging into her shoulder. She didn't want to think about it, but there was something wet beginning to soak through to her dress, the one Mrs. Appley had given her to wear, now that she wasn't Joe Bell anymore.

Hard telling who she was these days — Joe Bell . . . Afrika . . . Frieda . . . dead . . . alive. This wasn't blackness, it was nothingness. She began to tremble. Afrika squeezed her eyes shut, but this time, she felt lost at the edge of a swirling world.

Then she heard a hollow chatter from below,

and the vibrations of the bridge planks rumbled up through the wagon and into the casket. The dead man did a leaden jig beneath her. They both bounced wildly. Afrika braced herself against the pine sides of the box. It wouldn't be long now. There would be a service in a church. The minister said he was making it quick. They were to remove the casket through a rear door. They would stop so the widow could have one last look in private. And that was when Afrika would get out.

"Blessed be the Lord God." This must be it, Afrika thought. The minister had said that when she heard these words, she would know he had begun the benediction.

She felt the casket being lifted and carried down some steps. It seemed to take forever. She heard the minister's voice asking people to respect the widow's wishes for one last look at her dearly beloved husband. Afrika heard the double doors of a room shut. Quick footsteps followed. The lid was lifted, and two faces beamed down upon her.

"Bless you, child," said the woman. "To think

that I should find such life within death, such joy mixed with my deepest sorrow."

Afrika blinked. She wanted to bless every particle of light, every dust mote. That her freedom should be someone's joy seemed the most miraculous blessing of all.

Chapter 22

April 28, 1858

At the home of Thomas Garrett,
Wilmington, Delaware

Afrika stared down at her toes. They poked out of shoes that were little better than shreds laced onto her feet.

"Yes, dear, I do believe that a new pair is in order here. How about this nice sturdy pair of Moulton's? Never heard of anyone getting a blister from a well-fitted pair of Moulton's. 'Course in the shoe business, half of the challenge is in the fitting."

Thomas Garrett spoke softly as he helped Afrika out of her old shoes and into the new ones. They were in the hidden back room of his home in Wilmington. He was a shoe merchant, and on the second floor landing of his home behind a wall of shoe boxes and books there was a hidden door.

Afrika had looked in wonder as he removed

two books and revealed a shiny brass doorknob. He had fitted out with shoes hundreds of fugitive slaves who passed through his "waiting room" on the Underground Railroad. As he fitted the shoe, he told Afrika in his precise and soft voice how she would complete the rest of her journey to freedom, beyond the border and into Canada.

She would rest two days here at Garrett's in the hidden room. "The path just outside the city is well worn, and thee cannot miss it. An hour's good walking in new shoes will bring thee to the highway. Thee shall see a signpost, a wooden one, that marks the line between Delaware and Philadelphia. I shall give thee money. Thee must make thy way to the harbor. There thee will find a brig. Its name is the *Cameo.*"

At that point Thomas Garrett drew a piece of paper from his pocket. The name of the ship was printed in bold black letters. "I know thee does not read, but thee must study these letters in order to recognize the name on the hull of the ship. This ship is bound for Boston, out of Savannah with a cargo of pine lumber."

He continued to describe in detail how Afrika should look for a sailor who would be waiting near one of the massive bollards used for tying up ships and how he would help secrete her on board. Then he tapped the paper with the name CAMEO, and spoke intensely. "This is the most important word thee can learn now for the rest of thy life, Afrika." He bent forward, his clear gray eyes steady. "But it is not the last. It is only one of many words to come."

Afrika did not blow out her candle, but she let it burn down that night. She lay in the bed for hours, staring at the shapes of the letters, softly repeating the word they made. She fell asleep with the sound on her lips and the letter shapes in her dreams.

Afrika looked down at her feet in the brand-new shiny shoes Mr. Garrett had given her. She took the point of her shoe and traced a small C in the dust — small, so no one could see it. Then she felt something loose in her shoe. She took it off and shook. A toe fell out, then another and another. "My toes! My toes!" she screamed as she looked at the blood spurting from her foot and the little chopped-off toes nestling in the dust. . . .

Steal away, steal away,
Steal away to Jesus.
Steal away, steal away home. . . .

*Afrika clamped her hands over her ears. That song.
"No, Mammee Bert. Don't go to Tuckeroo." But
then it wasn't Mammee Bert. It was her. Baking in
the sun, her arms pinioned against the barn wall.
Her legs spread and chained to rings in the ground.
Like a bug in a web, except the web was on her
back, and Old Master was weaving it with his bullwhip. She'd gone down when she had heard the
song, down to the pit school where there was learning and letters going on with slaves from other
plantations. A spy had told Master, and he was
waiting for her when she returned. He was beating
her good. Now came the last lash. The crack came,
and then a razor-sharp hiss. . . .*

*"Next time we cut something off you, Frieda!" he
screamed.*

Afrika woke up in a cold sweat. *This* was next
time. She stared at the wrinkled piece of paper
with the precious word in her hand. "It was a
dream," she whispered. "Master ain't going to get

me." Master had cut Old John's toes off for running and Sandy's finger for keeping reading. First time Afrika had been whipped real bad was because of going down to a pit school. But the next time she'd been whipped wasn't for reading. She'd given up on that. It was for not lying with the overseer, and he'd sent her to the whipping house where they gave her the spiderweb on her back. Better than having something cut off.

But this is next time, she thought, *and I am reading.* She stared hard at the paper and whispered each letter and its sound, and she slid those sounds together into the word. The word *CAMEO*.

Two nights later, the brig *Cameo* set its topsails, and with the wind on its quarter, she sailed smartly out of Delaware Bay.

In a locker in the foremost section of the bow, Afrika nestled amidst half a ton of iron chains. The chains were not for her, but for the massive anchors that would be lowered when they arrived in Boston Harbor.

Chapter 23

May 1, 1858

Boston, Massachusetts

Lucy sat crouched in the corner of the hansom as it jiggled down Charles Street. She dared not look out the window, for her grandfather had warned her that for fifty years the residents of Boston were used to seeing him drive about alone at odd hours on calls to the sick. It would not do for another person to be seen in his company.

If by some chance they were caught, Lucy was to draw out the scope and the other paraphernalia used for watching birds, since they were supposedly owling with a slight detour to the Harvard Medical College to pick up some papers he had forgotten.

Lucy had suggested that she should sit up right in the driver's seat beside her grandfather, for no one would dream that a conductor would take his own grandchild on such a mission. This was their second run together. The first had been ten days earlier.

They crossed Cambridge Street and headed down North Grove, turning into a small back way called Fruit Street behind the medical college. Lucy could smell the stink of the river and the flats less than a hundred yards away. She felt the carriage stop. A blurred figure suddenly stepped out from around the corner. It didn't take more than ten seconds. The door to the hansom swung open, and a large ragged heap was deposited on the seat by her grandfather and Henry Bowditch. Bowditch inhaled sharply as he spotted Lucy crouched in the corner.

"She knows. She found out." Levi Bradford spoke succinctly. "Lucy, give the gentleman your bonnet. Help him tie it on. He is ailing." He paused and looked at the ragged bundle. "Sir, if we are stopped, you just keep doing what you're doing now — chattering your teeth too much to talk. I am driving an ailing old woman to the Settlement House Sanitarium. That is our story."

Lucy stared at the bundle. Indeed, there was a chattering sound issuing from the ragged heap.

She peered into the folds of the dirty canvas wraps and blankets as she began to untie her bonnet. Immense feverish eyes stared out from a broken face. A dirty bandage leaking fluids covered his chin. Sunken cheeks made the bones protrude like those of the skeletons Lucy had seen in her grandfather's books. When Lucy slid back the blanket from his head, his teeth chattered through the cloth.

Carefully Lucy put the bonnet on his head. He raised one hand to help her with the ties, and Lucy was shocked to see that he was missing his index finger. Gently she pushed the hand down. "I can do this for you." Outside she heard her grandfather and Mr. Bowditch talking.

"Bad trouble in Connecticut, Lev. Phony station complete with phony agent."

"You don't say?"

"I'm afraid so. Our opponents are not satisfied merely to spy these days. This phony station stuff is spreading. Rumor has it that Pinkerton detectives might be sent out to try to find out where these false stations are, who's running them. Sorry to drag you out again so soon. I'll have a new horse and rig in two days, so you can take it easy.

Nice of the Betts here to lend their house for the cause," he said, nodding at the door behind them.

"The less transporting around to various stations in Boston the better," Levi Bradford said. "If we could get them straight off the ships with no stops, that would be perfect."

"Yes, well, they've got more constables than rats down on the wharves these days. In the meantime, this fellow, Abel is his name, is pretty sick. Got chewed by dogs, running a fever. It was a long row in from Boston Light. Bearse said there wasn't a breath of air out there. Cold on the water these spring nights."

"Well, I'll dose him quick now to bring down his fever. But we'd better be on our way."

"All right, Lev. Godspeed."

By the time they had crossed over the bridge to Cambridge and were heading west toward Concord, the man's chattering had stopped. Slumped in the corner opposite Lucy, he seemed to be dozing. But just as they turned off the Cambridge turnpike and on to the Lexington road, he stirred.

"Thank you for your bonnet, miss." The voice sounded ratchety, like a rusted hinge.

"You're . . . you're welcome, sir," Lucy stammered.

"What be your name, miss?"

"Lucy."

"Lucy." He said her name slowly. She could see a smile begin to spread. "I had a baby boy one time, and I named him Leonard. I done wrote the letter L in the dirt one day, and Massa saw it and done chop off my finger — he called it my pointing, my reading finger."

"No!" Lucy gasped. "They cut off your finger for reading?"

"Oh, indeed. They near have fits when we wanted to get book learning. More fingers and toes chopped off for letter learning than anything else. Now imagine them thinking they could cut that letter out of me by chopping my finger off?" He tapped Lucy's bonnet with the stump of his finger. "I done name my first child Leonard."

"That's nice," said Lucy. "Nice you named your son that."

"He was sold off long time past. I heard he was sold off to same plantation as Moses, so maybe he got up here with her. You know the Moses lady, don't you?"

"The Moses lady?" Lucy said, bewildered.

"Miss Harriet Tubman."

"Oh, yes." But in truth Lucy knew very little about her. She remembered her grandfather referring to the woman, and she had heard vague reports about her leading fugitive slaves from the South on the Underground Railroad, but she had seemed to Lucy as much a fantasy as the train that ran underground.

Lucy, however, was learning fast that none of it was fantasy. It was all as real as the broken-faced black man who sat shivering across from her with his stump of a finger and his love for the letter L.

Chapter 24
May 16, 1858

Brookdale Farm in Brookline,

Massachusetts

Lucy sat alone in a delicate chair near the edge of the tent and listened to the orchestra play a waltz. She plucked absently at her pale blue dress. It was a stupid dress, one with flounces, and her mother had insisted that Bridget fix her hair swept up, with little corkscrew curls cascading around her ears. So every time Lucy moved, the flounces bounced and the curls jiggled about so that she seemed to pulsate like some quivering blob of jelly.

She watched Daisy dancing with Edmund de Rosey. Daisy looked positively aglow. If she only knew about the turquoise lady, she probably would not be so radiant. But there was no way Lucy could warn anybody without revealing where she had been that night. And now it was more important than ever to be quiet about her comings and goings.

Pap had promised her another "owling" expedition. She believed that Pap was becoming used to her company on the runs. It had been more than two weeks since they had picked up Abel. She wondered if by now Abel was in Canada.

Pap couldn't be here to host the dance he was giving for Iris. He'd taken an awful summer cold, and Zephy had forbidden him to attend. Who knew how many cargoes of dates he had missed? Lucy sighed.

"Why so glum, Lucy?"

"Mr. Shaw!"

"Robert, please. We're probably cousins, remember? Come on, will you give me a dance?"

"Surely."

He put his hand on her waist and began to guide her around the dance floor. His touch was light but firm, and the music seemed to flow through him directly to her. He was easy to dance with, thank heavens. Should she say something about how stupid she thought her curls were, so he wouldn't think she would wear her hair this way on purpose? No, she supposed that would call even more attention to them.

"You seem to be concentrating on something, Lucy."

"Oh . . . oh, no, nothing."

"A pity your grandfather couldn't make it."

"Oh, yes, I do miss him. Have you finished your examinations at Harvard yet, Robert?"

"Weeks ago. But I'm sticking around a bit — helping cousin Francis Parkman transcribe some notes. His eyes have been beastly this spring. And then I've been helping Henricks catalogue his fossil collections over at the zoology museum."

"Pardon me. But may I have the next dance?" Lucy had not noticed that the music had ended, and here was Henry Van Schuyler, stepping between her and Robert. Glistening and pink, he was a sight to make Lucy's heart sink.

"Well, I guess that leaves me and Robert." Delphy laughed lightly.

"I can't let an evening pass without experiencing Lucy's curious sense of humor," Henry Van Schuyler said.

"What do you mean by that?" Lucy scowled.

"Only a compliment, my dear. You are the most refreshing creature about. You know we New Yorkers have a difficult time with the New England restraint, the Puritan piety, on occasion."

His hand pressed into the small of her back, and he was guiding her expertly around the dance floor with a considerable amount of grace for someone of his size.

"Then why do you come here so much? Oh dear!" Lucy gasped. She had not intended to be that rude. But Henry Van Schuyler merely threw back his head and laughed. "You see what I mean, dear Lucy. You are irrepressible."

At the edge of the tent she caught sight of Jeremy, her grandfather's driver, whispering to Harold, her grandfather's butler and footman at Brookdale. What was Jeremy doing here? Had Pap decided to come after all?

Jeremy drove the calash at breakneck speed. Lucy, holding tight to her father's hand, lurched against his shoulder. There were so many questions she wanted to ask him, but they were all unanswerable. He knew no more than she did.

Jeremy had arrived with an urgent message that Pap's fever had suddenly soared, and his condition was — what had been the word? — "precarious." Jeremy had actually come to fetch Dr. Warren, Levi Bradford's personal physician, who was also attending the party. Now Dr. Warren sat across from them in stony silence. They had slipped out of the party almost unnoticed. Lucy's father did not want any undue disruption. The party must go on.

Finally they pulled up to 154 Beacon. Mary, their scullery maid, was waiting for them.

"Zephyra is upstairs," she said. Her face was blotchy, as if she had been crying.

They made Lucy wait outside the bedroom. It was half an hour before Zephyra came out, her face buried in her handkerchief.

"What is it, Zephyra? What is it? Why won't they let me in? I want to see Pap."

"He done have an apoplectic stroke now," Zephyra sobbed.

"What? I thought it was a cold, pneumonia."

"It was, but now he done have an apoplexy. Dr.

Warren looked at his eyes. They're like little pin-pricks, and he can't move his left side."

Soon Dr. Warren and her father came out, their faces heavy and gray. "I . . . I . . . don't know, Sherbourne. It's very dangerous. These clots, you can only hope they dissolve and do not pass to someplace more dangerous. There is nothing we can do but wait. It would be mad to move him. Any jostle could make the thing tear lose. I'm afraid at his age it doesn't look too hopeful."

"Papa?" Lucy called softly. Her father turned around and blinked.

"Lucy?" He spoke as if startled by her presence.

"Pap — is he going to die?"

"I . . ." Slowly he shook his head from side to side. "I don't know. You must run along to bed now, Lucy."

"Papa, I can't. Please, let me see him, please."

"Well . . ." Her father turned to Dr. Warren.

"No harm in it, I suppose."

At that moment Zephyra reappeared. Her tears had dried.

"Zephy, take Lucy in to see her grandfather."

* * *

Lucy was transfixed when she saw her grandfather stretched beneath the sheets in the massive bed. Something had happened to him. It was as if another person lay there. He was so gaunt he looked like a skeleton. The sheets seemed to outline every bone. His rib cage heaved under his labored breathing, but his body was strangely limp. One side of his face was pulled into ugly lines so that the left side of his mouth seemed to slide off his chin. His right eye was wide open and stared blankly at the ceiling while the left eyelid dropped.

"Pap," Lucy whispered and approached the bed. She laid her hand gently on his. His hand reminded her of a dry leaf fallen from a tree. And his breath seemed to whistle through him with a strange rasping sound. "Pap," she whispered again. But there was no response.

"He can't hear, Lucy. He can't see." Zephyra put both hands lightly on her shoulders.

Lucy stayed through the night. There had been no improvement by the following morning, and it was clear Lucy would not move. Zephyra fixed up pallets for each of them to sleep on near the bed.

Lucy's father came and went. Lucy's mother and Delphy both came to try to coax her away, but there was no coaxing to be done.

"It could go on like this a long time," Emeralda said to her daughter.

Lucy did not know how to answer. What was that supposed to mean? Time had no meaning for her. She had to be reminded to eat. Sometimes she fell asleep but in quick catnaps — ten or twenty minutes — from which she awoke amazingly refreshed. And always with hope — hope that he would wake up, that the staring eyes would recognize her, that perhaps he might speak just a word.

She thought she could accept his death, but what she could not accept was this silent passage out of her world. It was not so much that she needed to say good-bye, but Pap needed to go with words, with sounds, with human voices. To go insentient seemed so lonely. She did not want Pap to be lonely in his passage. If only some glimmer of light would come into his eye, for if it did not, how should he know the way?

Her mother, her father, her sisters came and went, but Zephyra and she stayed. Then Zephyra came down with the same cold and had to retreat to her quarters. A nurse was hired, but the nurse, seeing that Lucy was always there, began to snore in an easy chair in the far corner of the bedroom. It was just Lucy, her grandfather, and death waiting patiently.

In the small, dimmest hours of the night, Lucy took to laying her cheek down on the pillow near her grandfather's head. She heard the ragged breath, but it no longer disturbed her. It was as if another voice came from other times — from their times on the *Winsome* sailing to the harbor islands, their times tramping through the woods out at Brookdale, their times in the library.

This was her Pap who had shown her the track of the bobcat in the snow and the flight of the great horned owl. This was her Pap who had taught her to steer a steady course in a following sea with twenty knots of wind in the rigging. This was her Pap who dispelled the mysteries of the human body and taught her how to navigate by the stars. This was her Pap who gave her buckskin instead of flounces, leather hunting hats instead of corkscrew curls. This was her Pap who now lay dying.

Just after midnight, a curious thing began to happen. It was as if the agony of the struggle began to wash from her grandfather's face. The lines that scored his cheeks and radiated from the corners of his eyes seemed to disappear. His skin became smoother, and Lucy had the uncanny sense that she was glimpsing her grandfather as a boy. His breathing, too, became easier, but he was in a deep, deep sleep. Finally, at dawn, death made its dim approach and took him by the hand. Lucy felt his hand slip from hers. And then he was gone, swift as a sloop over the horizon with a following breeze.

The wedding had to be postponed. There was simply no way they could wear mourning for less than four months. And then, again, it would have to be a somewhat "reduced" affair, which apparently meant, as far as Lucy could tell, that there would not be footmen in silk hosiery.

Reduced affair or not, one thing had not changed — the amount of talk about it. If anything, it had increased, for so many of the plans had to be changed. It seemed as if everyone talked more about the wedding than they did about Pap's death. But Lucy did not question any of it nor show a trace of annoyance. She liked wearing mourning — it made life easier. There were no decisions to be made about dresses, no question of corkscrew curls. She listlessly agreed to everything. When Iris suggested that an apricot cotton voile would be a more appropriate color, warmer for what would now be a winter wedding, Lucy merely agreed.

The sisters had been sitting in the music room embroidering the endless Dozens.

"Of course apricot would be too strong a color for Lucy in the summer, for a summertime wedding." Rose giggled and looked at Daisy.

"Rose! Don't you dare!" Daisy exclaimed.

"Why? Worried I might jinx it? Come on, Daisy!"

"Well, Edmund has said that he would love for me to come down to Beau Rivage when you and Elwyn and cousin Henry come in September. But you know I hate to go down there in these mourning rags."

"Surely by September Mama would let you wear gray," Delphinia offered.

"Gray? And all those Southern belles in their peach and rose and yellow, and with their famous magnolia complexions? I'll look exactly like . . . like . . ."

"Mrs. Adams," Rose said, and all of the girls

burst into giggles except Lucy, who had hardly been following the conversation.

"Beau Rivage?" She suddenly looked up from the very neat line of stitches she had completed.

"Edmund's plantation," Daisy answered. "Are you back among the living, Lucy? I declare you have been so distracted since Grandfather died."

"Why would you be going to Beau Rivage?" Lucy asked with confusion.

"Because he invited her, silly," Iris said. "Remember when Elwyn invited me to Newport?"

"But that was the summer before you became engaged."

"Precisely," Rose said.

Lucy let her embroidery drop into the basket by her feet and stood up slowly. She looked at her sisters. Each one had a look of bemused merriment, almost indulgence, as they returned her gaze. These were the older sisters amused by their younger sister's simplicity, her innocence. But the irony was that they didn't know what she knew — that it was unthinkable Daisy should marry Edmund de Rosey. How could she ever tell Daisy what she had seen behind the Boston Theater? It would give away her own secrets, but if it would save Daisy. . . . Although Daisy was far from her favorite sister. On the other hand, the idea of her marrying such a man, who consorted with actresses while supposedly courting her. . . . All these thoughts were going through Lucy's mind when Daisy began speaking directly to her.

"And, Lucy, Edmund says, as Mama has so often said, that referring to your own grandfather as Pap is a very pickaninnish thing to do. Little slave children call old men Pap down at Beau Rivage."

Delphinia shifted her eyes nervously. "But Lucy always called Grandfather Pap."

"But now that Grandfather is gone, perhaps she could fall in line with the rest of us and call him . . ." Daisy stopped speaking. Indeed all of the sisters froze. Lucy stood dark and glowering.

"Daisy, if Mr. Edmund is so set on proper manners and does not take to my manner of speaking, perhaps he should first look to his own."

Daisy's mouth set into a grim little line, and her pale gray eyes became icy cold. Iris stood up and fretted with the embroidery hoop in her hands.

"Now, dear Lucy, if you're referring to the words about Mr. de Rosey's card habits that had disturbed Father, that just isn't so, or at least not anymore. Mr. de Rosey is very lucratively employed now, representing Southern interests in the North. I'm not quite sure what it is, but Elwyn and Henry both assure us it is quite respectable and makes a handsome profit."

Lucy looked hard at her sisters. Here was Daisy falling for the handsome and "beautifully mannered" Edmund de Rosey. And Delphy had definitely gone sweet on Henry Van Schuyler. What would she say if she knew about Dulcey and Henry?

It suddenly struck Lucy that Daisy and all her sisters were in some ways like compasses with no northing. She must put an end to their delusions.

"Well . . ." She spoke so softly that each sister had to strain to listen. "I was not referring to those 'words' about his card playing, but others." She paused. A shadow crossed Daisy's face.

"What words?" asked Delphinia.

"Apparently Mr. de Rosey has been seen about with a certain red-haired actress who appears on the stage of the Boston Theater."

Lucy never got to the part about Henry and Dulcey. An embroidery hoop sailed through the air and smacked Lucy on the jaw. "I shan't believe it! I shan't!" Daisy cried. "You little witch! Spiteful thing. You have always been the most spiteful child."

But the damage was done. The "word" need only be breathed. Iris, Delphinia, and Rose knew that although she was different, Lucy never lied. They also knew that she was closest to the housemaids, and this was the sort of gossip that scullery maids and serving girls would pass along.

Lucy touched her jaw where the hoop had hit her. It would sound feeble if she said she was sorry to Daisy, for she wasn't. But she would be very sorry if Daisy did marry such a man. "I think, Daisy . . ."

"You have thought enough, Lucy. Why don't you go to your room."

Lucy cast her eyes down. "I was going to say, Daisy, that if these rumors were proved untrue, in my heart I know you deserve better than Edmund de Rosey."

Quiet enveloped the room, and long shafts of

late afternoon sunlight shot through the immense arched windows. No one spoke a word.

Lucy gathered her workbasket and left the music room. *Pap,* she thought. *I shall always call him Pap.*

Chapter 26

June 15, 1858

One mile south of Boston Light,

Massachusetts

It was a still and starless summer night. There was not a breath of wind. A fog bank loomed on the horizon. A brigantine, its canvas flapping in the lethargic rhythms that drive homebound sailors to distraction, wallowed in the swells off Boston Light.

In Afrika's mind, the gale of two days ago was preferable to this. Bent, the sailor who had helped her every day she had been in the chain well, had said if they did not make Boston Light well before midnight, they could not off-load her until the next evening. Boston was a dangerous place now, he said. The constables scoured the wharves and the piers and often obtained search warrants for vessels coming from the South.

"Tell me," whispered Afrika. "Do the stars show tonight?"

"No, no," Bent said. "And I daresay it is going to be thick-a-fog soon enough. Could help yuh, though. Maybe we could off-load yuh in a real pea souper. Nobody'd see a thing!"

"Pea souper?" Afrika asked.

"Just an expression. Fog come in so thick. We say thick as mud down east, Port Clyde. They say pea soup u't'here in Bean Town."

Afrika bit her lip lightly as she contemplated the strange words and rhythms of Bent's talk. She had never heard anyone talk this way. He was a Mainer, and their manner of speech was peculiar. "How come you call Port Clyde down when it ain't south but north, and what's this bean town?"

"Boston, gal! Don't you know that?"

Afrika shook her head.

"They call it Bean Town 'cause that about all they eat here — beans and cod. And Maine ain't up from here but down, down east, cause that the way the wind blows most of the time — a following breeze. Blows on yuh quarter so yuh can run down wind all the way to Maine."

Bent was a practical man, and he always came up with sound, practical reasons for anything he did. He had shown Afrika what he called the simple sense behind a dozen or more fancy knots. He had even shown her how to weave a pillow from the shredded ends of the ropes used for hoisting sails. Now she arranged that pillow on the mountain of iron chain that had become her bed, her home, her world, for over a month. Due to poor winds and unexpected repairs, the voyage had taken three times as long as expected. Afrika said good night to Bent, and he promised to fetch her when the time came.

Toward midnight, Afrika crawled over the heaps of chain to the hawsehole, through which the line ran when the anchor was lowered. This had been her only view of the world beyond the ship for the past several weeks. But now her heart sank, for although it was midnight, that world had turned milky white with fog.

So this was a pea souper. Even if they had made Boston Light by midnight, how would anybody find them in this thick fog? For the first time in many weeks, her hopes began to dwindle. She pressed her cheek against the hawsehole, nearly desperate to see the fog thin. But it remained, reminding her of an old slave at Marlymont whose eye had turned milky blue and finally disappeared under a thick coating of white.

The night was as blind as that old slave's eye, and no one would ever find her or the brig *Cameo*. It became almost suffocating, this fog. But there was something hypnotizing about the thick, swirling whiteness, and soon Afrika was transfixed. She simply could not take her eye from the hawsehole. And a strange transformation began to occur within her. The panic that had seized her gut, the sickly taste in the back of her throat, began to disappear, and a calmness stole over her. She discovered a new place within her.

Afrika was not sure if this place was within her mind, her heart, her soul, or her spirit. But she felt a presence out there. She knew as surely as she had known anything that someone was coming for her. She did not need to see this person. She did not need to hear him. But she knew he was there.

And she was right. Austin Bearse stood at the helm of his small yacht, *Pilgrim Girl*. Bearse was accustomed to fog. His eyes read it like some nocturnal animal prowling the darkest jungle. His sloop moved like a ghost through the night.

A gentle breeze had come up, perfect for a small racing yacht, yet barely putting a wrinkle into the canvas of the *Cameo*. It was not the first time Bearse had been sent for a special cargo; whenever the dates came in by sea, he was the one dispatched. Yet once, many years before, he had delivered slaves for auction.

A few years after his slave delivery, Bearse first saw an issue of *The Liberator,* the abolitionist paper of William Lloyd Garrison. After he read it, he began to make contact with other abolitionists and soon dedicated his life to helping fugitive slaves. Using a series of small yachts, he had delivered many a "cargo" to freedom.

Tonight it had been Wendell Phillips who had sought him out. The message had come through that afternoon — the arrival of a cargo of dates was imminent. What with the last two cargoes being seized right out from under their noses, they were now going to have to move with extreme caution.

The emergency meeting of the Vigilance Committee had been called for just this purpose, to try to find ways to elude the newly strengthened network of spies and infiltrators from the South. The old pathways and routes, even some of the stations, were no longer secure. Codes were being cracked, stations discovered. They had heard of false stations operating in Connecticut and Rhode Island. Now there were rumors of ones in the Boston area. Pinkerton agents had been sent in to help detect false stations, but so far neither they nor the committee had been able to discover where the rumored stations actually might be.

Afrika felt a joy well up within her. For although she could not put a name to Austin Bearse, nor ever know his history, she felt his presence. There was in this night someone coming, coming to help her. Despite the flap of the *Cameo*'s sails and the groans and creaks of her timbers, Afrika's eyes widened as she heard another sound — the soft whisper of a light boat on a gentle wind.

"Ahoy there!" a voice called out from the very throat of the fog.

Feet scuffled, and greetings were exchanged.

The men of the brig responded as Bearse supposed they would — thinking that anyone on a small sailing yacht was in some sort of trouble to be sailing at midnight through a fog.

"Are you in need of help?"

"No, Captain. I am perfectly fine," Bearse answered cheerily. "I just came up from the cape."

"Are you lost?" The captain pressed anxiously as he peered over the rail at the small boat.

"Indeed not. Are you?" This drew a hearty laugh from the crew.

"No, sir. I know my way about these Noddle flats 'tween here and the Governor's Flats."

"Sir!" Bearse did not need to exaggerate the alarm in his voice.

"Yes?"

"You're nowhere near Noddle Flats."

"What?"

"You're off Brewster Bar to starboard of Ram's Head, as well you should leave it. There's been a tremendous amount of silting in the last month. You have a pilot coming out, I assume?"

"Not till dawn." At that moment the breeze picked up, and there was a noisy flapping of canvas.

"Sir, should we hoist the tops?"

"Don't interrupt me, Smyth, when I'm con-versing." The captain then called down to Bearse. "How well do you know these waters, sir?"

"Sir, I come out for pleasure in my yacht in the fog — I 'spect I know them pretty well."

"Well, I don't take to hanging around here flap-ping my sails when there's a wind to catch. Would you be interested in piloting me in? I'll pay you standard wage plus some."

"Ah . . ." Bearse paused. "It's not a question of money, sir. It's my yacht. She's a pretty little thing, and who's to mind my *Pilgrim Girl*?"

"No problem, sir. We'll throw you a hawser." Bearse could barely conceal his disgust. These captains! Where did they come from now-adays — Indiana? A hawser would rip the fine teak planks right out of his deck.

"Well, some lighter cordage might do better, Captain, but to tell you the truth, if you have a good down-easter on board, well, him I might trust with my helm."

"Well, by Jove, you're in luck, sir. We got such a lad on board. Smyth, find Bent."

"Right here, Captain." A voice rang out in the fog.

"Can you take the helm of this kind man's yacht?"

"Ayuh," replied Bent with a nod.

The single word was music to Bearse's ears. He knew he had his man. He had been told that the contact was a down-easter from Port Clyde, Maine.

"Send over a ladder, mates," the captain ordered.

As soon as Bent's feet touched the deck, he was whispering to Bearse. "She's waiting at the first porthole after the hawsehole. She don't know how to swim and is scared to death. You tell them you want to back the sail and bring *Pilgrim Girl* about to show me how these running backstays work."

"Of course I do. You think I'm going to let any dumb cluck, even barring clever lads from Port Clyde, handle my *Girl* without proper instruction?"

Bearse then shouted up to the captain, "Sir, I beg a minute here to show this fellow how things work. I'll just ghost forward a bit to demonstrate the mechanics for moving the starboard backstay, in case we get a wind shift."

The captain muttered something to himself. He supposed he had to be patient. These yachtsmen were all alike, finicky fellows.

Afrika slid halfway out of the porthole. She gripped its lip with her hands, and her toes found the half-inch projection on the side of the ship. She did not know it, but she stood on top of the letter C, the first letter of the ship's name, which had been carved and nailed to the hull rather than painted. But now she was terrified. She could hear the water lapping at the sides of the ship, but she could not see it. All was still white. She could see nothing.

"Drop!" hissed a voice beneath her. "Drop, Afrika. If you don't drop, we'll slide right by you. You must drop now! Drop or drown!"

"Dear God!" she moaned.

She dropped.

"Are you all right, child?" A large, grizzled-looking man stood over her. She nodded, still stunned by her fall and the ache in her knees where she had hit. "There's no time to waste. These fools couldn't find their way to Boston in broad daylight let alone in a night like this."

Quickly they stuffed Afrika down the forward hatch of the *Pilgrim Girl.*

"Well, I think you've got the hang of the back-stays, son. See you as soon as we safely deliver *Cameo* to within striking distance of the wharf. I'll rejoin you then." With that, Bearse turned and began climbing the ladder to the *Cameo.* So far, so good, he thought. Now if they could just avoid the spies.

"Gentlemen," Bearse said as he swung his large legs over the rail. "I am your pilot."

Chapter 27

June 16, 1858

Boston, Massachusetts

Sometime between the last meeting of the Vigilance Committee at 21 Cornhill Road and the delivery to the Underground Railroad station at the base of Beacon Hill, a word had been misspoken or perhaps heard wrongly.

Afrika had been amply warned of the perils of spies, informants, and false stations. The Griswold house at 14 Biron Street had been expecting the shipment of dates, not just plain dates, but rather those from the Levant. According to the code, they had sent Afrika on through the hidden tunnel that commenced in their basement. The tunnel could be traversed only at certain hours, as the lower part of it was subject to flooding from the tidal waters of the Back Bay. During this particular week, the spring tides had begun. These tides were extreme and could cut off the first third of the underground passageway.

Afrika saw vestiges of this tide as she began the walk that would take her one-half mile underneath the streets of Boston. Within the first minute, she discovered the carcass of a fish. Crabs and rats scuttled across the path. She carried a small lantern, but as she soon discovered, it had a troublesome wick, and every fifty feet or less she had to stop to fix it so it would not extinguish itself.

Once there had been turnoffs, but these had been sealed. There was no possibility of a wrong turn now. She would know she was nearing the end when she reached a very steep incline. The path would pitch up sharply for fifteen feet, or a bit less. At the top of the incline, there would be a small wooden door — quite small. She would be forced to crouch down and squeeze through it.

This was why the pathway could only be used by fugitives of a certain size. Once through the wooden door, she would come to the lath of an interior wall. The lath had been cut away quite precisely, and what appeared to be the rear of a large cabinet would be facing her. She should step into this cabinet. She would find a small seat, and if she pressed her knees together, she should be able to sit in relative comfort until the agent came. This was a reliable station. There had been some changes recently. However, it was anticipated that the station would be running smoothly by the time Afrika arrived.

The wick in Afrika's lantern began to sputter again. She stopped, crouched, and tried to poke it with the stick she had found. A rat paused to study her. "Get!" she hissed. Then the wick was extinguished. Total darkness. She felt panic well up in the back of her throat. What would she do now?

Afrika had been in total darkness before. There had been the coffin. This was not as bad as that. She remembered the velvet blackness of the night woods, which she had come to cherish and to seek. And then she recalled that other darkness from long ago, the one with the plum sheen that came from the heart of Mammee Bert's blackness. But this wasn't that kind of black. She suddenly remembered a dusky old man with night-blue skin. He was missing part of a finger. She supposed he'd been caught reading, tracing letters with his fingers or something.

She groped her way, her hands feeling along the clammy walls. Finally she reached the incline. She began to scrabble up.

Soon she felt the wood of the door. Carefully she opened it. She hoped that Mr. and Mrs. Griswold were right about this house. Suddenly all the talk of spies and false stations flooded through her. She felt her heart race as she squeezed through the small doorway. Did she really have any choice? They had to be right. But what if they were spies themselves? Well, then, why wouldn't they have sent her back right away?

At that moment, Afrika was more frightened than she had ever been since she had left Marlymont. In the dim light she could see the lath of the wall cut away, just as the Griswolds had described. She could see the opening at the back of the cabinet and the small seat nailed into its side. She could turn back.

But no, she couldn't, for the Griswolds were leaving that evening, and the tunnel entrance to their house would be locked. The tide would be turning. The realization dawned on her. She had no choice. If she turned back, she would drown.

Chapter 28

June 17, 1858

154 Beacon Street,

Boston, Massachusetts

Lucy sat at her grandfather's desk. Since the unpleasant events in the music room, Lucy had begun to spend more and more time at 154 Beacon. Often she would spend the night in her father's old bedroom. Her parents were used to it and had given up fighting her on this issue. Even though Zephy was still away sick, Jeremy was always there. It seemed to be where Lucy was happiest.

Within the last hour, Lucy had made an amazing discovery. If only Zephyra were here. But her pneumonia had lingered on, and Lucy's parents had sent her out to Cape Ann for the fresh salt breezes. Zephy, Lucy was sure, could have explained the confounded train schedules she had just found, but now Lucy herself was beginning to detect a pattern.

First, she had been surprised when she had discovered the train and stagecoach schedules in Levi Bradford's desk. Her grandfather rarely took a train or a coach, and in her memory he had never traveled on the Baltimore & Ohio. She had guessed that these schedules were not concerned with aboveground travel but had something to do with the Underground Railroad.

The one for the Boston-Concord-Fitchburg coach line was very tattered. But the circled numbers seemed to have no rhyme or reason. She sat very still and wondered. Perhaps the numbers did not correspond to times at all, had nothing, in fact, to do with times. Could they mean number of passengers or packages? 2:00 P.M. She stared hard at the numbers on the Boston-Concord coachline schedule.

Suddenly a stone marker flashed in her mind. She had seen the number 2 on it. Yes, the evening she had gone with her grandfather to deliver the man named Abel to a house on the Lexington road. They had turned off the Cambridge turnpike, and before the house came up, there had been a mile marker with the number 2 on it. If one had continued another mile, which would be mile marker 3, one would find Bronson Alcott's home and, nearby, Pap's friend Mr. Emerson.

Sure enough, there were two circles around the 3:00 on the schedule. For Pap had told her that the Alcotts and the Emersons helped out, too, and were stations on the Underground.

Quickly, she seized a Boston-Maine schedule. This could be the test for her theory. So intent was she that she did not hear the soft thump on the other side of the room. She had Bowditch's address and, of course, she knew the Charles Francis Adamses on Mount Vernon. Bowditch's number was 40. She ran her finger down the schedule. Indeed! 4:00 was circled. Where did he live but 40 Clarendon? But the real proof was the numeral 1, beside which was a small circle with a curved mark coming out of the top. An apple and the numeral 1 stood for the single address on Fruit Street behind Harvard Medical College.

It was the only building that resembled a house at all, and it was in front of this building that she and her grandfather had met Mr. Bowditch and Abel. Yes, and now she recalled they had met him there because Bowditch's horse and rig were not up to the trip that night. If they had been, they probably would have taken Abel over to Clarendon.

Another thump and a scratching noise could be heard across the room. Lucy jerked her head up from the schedules.

She looked over at the huge grandfather clock. Its hands were still frozen at two o'clock. Two o'clock! Suddenly Lucy felt the world she knew begin to dissolve.

In the past few minutes, as she had studied the train schedules, things, objects, words, and numbers began to slip from their moorings, to have acquired new meanings. Nothing was as it seemed. Railroads no longer ran aboveground, but under, and the hours of their arrivals and departures no longer signified time, but places. Simple words like apples and dates acquired dramatic new meanings.

Lucy stood up as if in a trance and felt herself drawn to the clock on the east wall. She knew its history. And she knew how it had been given to her grandparents and had worked for just five minutes although their marriage had lasted more than fifty years. And then she heard a sigh from behind its rich mahogany panel. The clock *was* working!

She turned the key that opened the panel so the clock could be wound. But since it had never worked, it had probably never been wound. And in fact there was nothing to wind. The entire innards of the clock were gone, and in the place where brass gears and weights would have been, there sat a girl the color of the great clock itself. A mahogany girl. She was a deep, deep brown-black, and under the rich darkness of her skin was a sheen of red.

"Are you a spy? If you are, just kill me right now. I'm tired of running."

Chapter 29

June 17, 1858

154 Beacon Street,

Boston, Massachusetts

Time had stopped for both girls. They stared at each other, drinking in every detail of the other girl's face, posture, expression.

Lucy was unsure how old the dark-skinned girl was. Was she fourteen — her own age — or maybe just a bit older, fifteen or sixteen? She had beautifully molded lips. They were a lighter color than her skin, but just at their edges was a faint, dusty pink. The girl's eyes were tilted ever so slightly, and her silky eyebrows were thick and well shaped. Her forehead was high. Her hair was pulled back tightly into a bun. She seemed terribly thin, but she was in better condition than Abel had been. She cocked her chin and peered hard at Lucy.

"Well, are you?"

"Am I what?"

"A spy."

"A spy for what?"

"A spy for slave catchers."

"Certainly not! My grandfather, Levi Bradford, was the stationmaster here, but . . . but . . ." Lucy was confused. Pap had been an agent, but had he actually been a stationmaster? Was 154 Beacon a real station on the Underground Railroad? Was this how the fugitives arrived when they came to his house?

"Where is he?" Afrika asked.

"He's dead."

"Dead? Well, Mrs. Griswold said there'd been some changes here."

Afrika stopped; she looked at Lucy. The dark fabric of Lucy's dress made her look unnaturally pale despite a flush in her cheeks. This could not be the person who was supposed to open the cupboard door. She didn't look old enough, strong enough, steady enough, to do a thing. The child was quivering like a leaf, and her eyes were darting all over the room.

"How in heaven's name did you get here?" Lucy asked.

"It's a long story. . . ." Afrika sighed. "I run way from Marlymont last Christmas."

"I don't mean that. I mean how did you get here — into Pap's study, into that clock?"

"Clock?"

"That's what you're sitting in."

Afrika leaned out of the clock and then stood up. "Well, I'll be . . ."

"But how did you get in there?"

"You mean you don't know?" Afrika asked with alarm in her eyes.

"Of course I don't know, or I wouldn't be asking."

"What's your name, miss?" Afrika asked.

"Lucy. And what is yours?"

"Afrika."

"Afrika!" Lucy repeated the name, her voice soft with wonder. "Afrika. You are named for a continent."

A continent? She knew she had been named for the place that her mother's people had come from.

"What does your name mean?" Afrika asked quietly.

Lucy smiled. "I never knew until my grandfather told me a few months ago, before he died. It means light."

"Light!" Afrika said. "Like a star?"

"Yes, light or shining."

"Like the North Star."

"Well . . ." Lucy hesitated. Her grandfather had told her how the fugitives navigated their way north by following the Big Dipper, the Drinking Gourd they called it, which points to the North Star.

Afrika cocked her head and looked at Lucy.

"About the clock," Lucy pressed. "Can you tell me how you arrived here through this clock?" She walked up to the clock and peered in. "Why, there's no back, and the wall behind has been cut away."

"Yes," Afrika said, and then she began to tell Lucy about the tunnel that led from the Griswolds on Biron to the house she found herself in now. She was not one to talk much, and the effort made her even more tired.

Lucy checked the schedule again. There was a six circled across from the Boxford stop on the Boston and Maine railroad line. She had begun to suspect that the names of the stops somehow related to the names of the streets of the numbered addresses, for only certain numbers in certain columns were circled. She did not know the exact number of the Griswolds' address on Biron, but she would bet it was six. There was quite a bit to the code that she did not have the time now to figure out. And there was so much to figure out in this labyrinthine world of the Underground Railroad.

"What am I to do?" Afrika said aloud.

Lucy had been wondering the same thing herself. What were they supposed to do now? If Zephy were here, she would know. But Zephy wasn't here. She was in Cape Ann. Lucy was unsure if Jeremy had been a party to her grandfather's activities.

The evening shadows were gathering. Lucy looked again at the train schedule, the one with the little apple drawn beside the number one. There was no one to tell her what to do. But she was a practical person. The logical conclusion that she came to was to take this girl to number 1 Fruit Street, because hadn't Mr. Bowditch said it was a good place in case of emergencies, and the Betts were so nice about everything? This was an emergency.

Chapter 30
June 17, 1858
Boston, Massachusetts

The two figures made their way down Charles Street. The one behind was laden with hat boxes and packages. To anyone passing by, they appeared to be a young mistress returning from a shopping expedition with her personal maid.

Lucy had dressed up Afrika in one of Zephyra's coal-scuttle bonnets and light capes. Her fresh apron showed beneath. They walked to the end of Charles Street, crossed Cambridge, and threaded their way through the smaller, less noticeable alleyways that laced the west end of Boston. Within a few minutes they were on Fruit Street.

Lucy sniffed and crinkled her nose. "The bay stinks tonight."

The tide was on the rise, and all Afrika could

think of was how awful it would have been to have been trapped in the tunnel.

Fruit Street was totally deserted. Lucy wondered what kind of people the Bettses were to want to live in the dark shadows of the medical college, so near the stench of the bay. They must work for Harvard, she concluded, custodians or the like. The whole area gave her a creepy feeling when she remembered that they were very near the dissecting laboratories. She tried not to think about it now. She took a deep breath, walked briskly up to the door, and rapped.

They waited for a few moments, and then she rapped again. Almost immediately they heard footsteps. The latch turned, and then the door swung open. Lucy was prepared to greet Mr. or Mrs. Betts, whom she had never met, but she was astonished when she saw the freckled face of a young woman.

"Dulcey!"

"Miss Lucy!" the young woman replied, equally astonished.

Lucy couldn't imagine what Dulcey was doing here. It was almost as odd as imagining Dulcey at the Jellicoe Gardens, drinking champagne with Henry Van Schuyler. Why was she not at the Philipots', where she worked? Perhaps she was related to the Bettses?

Dulcey evidently wondered the same about Lucy, for this was not what she was expecting, either.

"Are . . . are . . . are you fr — " she began to say.

But Afrika had heard it often enough over the last several months. "She is a friend with a friend."

Dulcey looked slightly relieved. "Oh, yes, and do come in."

She ushered them into the kitchen. "Would you like something to eat?"

"Yes," Afrika answered quickly, for she had not eaten in many hours. They sat at a crude kitchen table while Dulcey went to the larder. All the time she talked, often lapsing into a stutter that Lucy had never noticed before.

"She's very nervous, I think," Lucy said, leaning forward and whispering to Afrika. Dulcey came back into the room with some cold meat and a plate of cookies.

"Are Mr. and Mrs. Betts here?" Lucy asked. "I must talk to them, for a message must be sent so we can get Afrika on her way."

"Yes, yes, of course." Dulcey coughed nervously. "The problem is that they aren't here right now."

"Where are they?"

"Well, I'm not sure, but they did leave instructions that . . . that . . . that I was suppose to send a message over . . . over . . . over . . ."

"To Cornhill, no doubt. You see," Lucy continued, "I think there must have been a slight mix-up." She leaned forward and tried to speak as knowingly as possible. "The parcel, the dates from the Levant, well, I'm sure that they thought Zephrya could take care of dispersing them since my grandfather has passed, but she's not there at the moment. She's away."

"Not there . . ." Dulcey let the words hang.

"Yes, I imagine they didn't know that, and . . ."

Dulcey smoothed back her hair. She seemed to regain some composure. "Well, don't trouble yourself, miss. I have precise instructions from the Bettses as to the sending of a message for parcel deliveries, and this can be taken care of. Just rest yourself here a piece. Would you care, perhaps, for some tea to go with that? I have a kettle going. You know Mum always says that a hot drink on a hot summer day does as much to cool one down as anything. Odd, isn't it, but true." She blinked. Her eyes were fiercely bright. She poured their tea, offered them some cookies, and sat with them for a minute while they ate and drank. Then she set off to go carry the message.

As soon as she was out of earshot, Afrika leaned over and touched Lucy's hand.

"We should leave."

"What?" said Lucy. "What are you talking about?" She had been lost in thought about the code, but now it was not the code of the train schedules but the word "dates." She wondered if perhaps there were two kinds of dates — regular dates and fruit from the Levant. And if "Levant" was not a code for her grandfather Levi, then wouldn't it be possible for a slip to occur just in speaking, and for the dates to go to the wrong station?

"I don't trust her," Afrika said.

"Don't trust her? Dulcey isn't a devious sort. She's much too simple." So simple that she was impressed with that swine of a man at the Jellicoe Gardens.

"That don't make no difference, Miss Lucy," Afrika said firmly.

"No, Afrika, I have just now figured it all out. You see there's a code . . . and . . ." She was going to explain about the dates and the mix-up with the people thinking that Zephy was there. But her tongue suddenly became so thick in her mouth that she could barely move it to speak. Afrika leaned forward as if to touch her hand again, but suddenly Afrika's hand felt like a leaden weight. "My arm is so . . ."

Afrika heard a voice. She knew that voice — Ida — what was Ida doing here in Boston? "I'm supposed to be in Boston, I'm north now." But no one heard her. I got Lucy. A star come down from heaven to lead me. This doesn't make sense. But then she saw little children running around the trough. They looked right through her.

"He going to come get you soon." It was Ida speaking. She ambled up in that loose way she had of walking. "You see all these little ones running around here, the ones that looks like they got the

red dust in their hair and the mealy coloring? Them's his."

"How come he ain't got you?"

"He did get me, gal. He jes didn't get no child on me. I'm barren and I'm too old now to be of interest. But now you're coming into your woman years. He going to bother you good, and you might as well do it. Close your eyes and do it, else he'll start thinkin' 'bout ways to mess you up and next thing you know he be sending you to the whipping house."

"No." But she couldn't move. She was too heavy to move.

She was struggling under an old weight now, an immense, crushing weight. She smelled his smell. He blotted out the sky, he sucked out her breath. Then it was over. She got good at hiding, but then he eventually discovered her.

"I told you there's no use refusing him." Ida's voice scratched the dusty air. "They going to dig a hole for that belly of yours."

She came home afterward with her back all torn up. For more than a week, Ida put the thick juice on it. At the end of ten days, she said, "Gal, you got yourself a spiderweb on your back."

* * *

Then Afrika felt her limbs lighten. She reached for the dark threads of her dream and began climbing out of her nightmare.

The air lay heavy. Words stirred thickly through the dark. Lucy tried to move her fingers. The message burned out somewhere between her brain and her hand. She could not even feel her fingers. They had melted together into one unfeeling mass. The same with her feet. The words came again from another space, another room.

A sharp crack of vertical light came from a door not completely closed. Lucy blinked. Then blinked again. Her hands and feet might be numb, but she was suddenly alert. Laudanum, or some strong sleeping draught. Of course! They had been drugged. It all came back to her now. Afrika had been right. They shouldn't have trusted Dulcey.

The door suddenly swung open. A gray-capped figure moved briskly into the room. *I must feign sleep,* Lucy thought. The figure moved closer. She bent over a heap that Lucy guessed was Afrika. Then she came toward Lucy.

Lucy closed her eyes. A cool hand touched her

cheek, then picked up her hand and dropped it. It fell like a deadweight. The woman moved to her foot. Lucy dared open her eyes just a slit. Through the fringes of her eyelashes, she could make out a face in the dim light. The woman was dressed like a Quaker. She picked up Lucy's left foot. Some feeling was returning, but Lucy let it drop heavily.

"Hmmph." Lucy could not tell if the small, short sound was one of approval or disapproval. A fiery red frizz of hair popped out from beneath the woman's cap. Lucy was stunned. It was the same woman she had seen on the outer stairway of the Boston Theater. And as if to confirm this, she heard a familiar drawl from the other room. "How're they doing, Goldie?"

Goldie! The Prairie Flower!

"Still out."

The light from the door was suddenly blocked. A languorous figure leaned against the jamb.

Lucy's mind swam with confusion. Despite the severely cut frock coat and plain shirt with no cravat, Lucy recognized Edmund de Rosey. So this was his new lucrative endeavor that her sisters had mentioned, the one that gave him the respectabil-

ity that cards could not. He was a slave catcher!
And Henry probably was, too. That was why he
had been wooing Dulcey.

Yes, it made sense. Henry was not the brightest.
He had been doing all right in the family banking
and brokerage business, but with his tastes for
pleasure and good food he needed supplemental
income. A poor relative of the Van Schuylers
would never rise as far in the firm as someone like
Elwyn. Slave catching — the perfect job for a
swine.

Lucy remembered the conversation between
her grandfather and Mr. Bowditch when they had
talked of the bad trouble in Connecticut — the
phony houses, the spies. Right now they were in a
false station. Perhaps once it had been safe, but it
was no longer, and standing in the doorway was a
spy. It was all too clear to Lucy. But then her train
of thought stopped. What was this he was saying?

"Damn that Henry! I thought I'd never shake
him. But then again, that might be a little too
much to hope for. The real point is, he can't be on
to this house till we clear them out. Then, my dear,
I'm off, out of here. I don't think I could stand another gluttonous dinner with that beast."

"He's your cousin, isn't he?"

"Well, yes, he is — from the poor branch. Never seemed to cultivate this cousinly relationship until Elwyn became engaged. Thought we could both find ourselves some rich Boston heiresses. As a matter of fact, he seemed quite aware of our third mortgage on Beau Rivage."

"Well, he's more smitten with good old Dulcey than any heiresses."

"Oh yes, indeed. But he plans to propose marriage to Delphinia Bradford and then hire Dulcey as a housekeeper."

"The pig!" Lucy nearly gasped out loud and quickly clapped her hand over her mouth. It was then she realized that feeling had crept back into her arms. And what did de Rosey plan to do? Marry Daisy and hire Goldie as a music teacher?

It was no use thinking about that now. There was only one thing that she must focus her mind on — escape. Feeling had begun to steal back into her toes as well as her fingers. She wondered how Afrika was doing.

"They are definitely out for another good bit." The woman spoke and turned to leave the room. "What will we do with Miss Blue Blood?"

"Don't worry about her. I want to fetch Constable Penn and get the darkie on the next schooner out. Her price is up to fifteen hundred. I'm going down to the wharves first to check. Too bad we missed the sailing of *The Pearl*. I'll find out when the next departure is and get hold of Penn."

The woman moved through the door, and they closed it. But Lucy heard de Rosey's last words. "Give me a couple of hours, three at most."

"You hear that?" The whisper came from the heap in the corner.

"You awake, Afrika?"

"I sure am."

"You were right about Dulcey."

"I'm not getting back on no ship. And I ain't going back to no Marlymont."

"I'm thinking . . . I'm thinking. How are your feet?"

She waited several seconds for an answer. "They're better. They sho' felt dead few minutes ago."

"Keep wiggling your toes. Then, when you're ready, try kneeling and putting a little weight on them. But we've got to be quiet."

"We got to get out of here. I don't see no window, and only one door."

"The man is leaving," Lucy paused. "I heard him say so."

"We can take care of that lady and the Dulcey girl ourselves."

Lucy wasn't exactly sure what Afrika meant by "take care of."

"You mean *kill them*?"

"I mean get them out of the way."

"Get them out of the way." The words had a strange resonance for Lucy. There was perhaps a clue, a key, a hidden meaning in them. Lucy's feet might be half numb, but she seemed to have a heightened awareness of other things. She knew, for example, that she was facing northeast. On the far side of the medical school was the Charles slip where the *Winsome* was moored. There were walls, there were buildings, there were two women — that was what stood between them and the *Winsome,* between them and freedom.

Afrika saw that Lucy was kneeling. "How are your feet?"

"Good. How are yours?"

"Let me see." Slowly Afrika rose to a crouching

position, then gently rocked back, putting weight on her feet. She stood up. She looked about.

There was only one way out of this room, and they were going to need a weapon. Afrika scanned the space. On top of a small stove was an iron resting on a trivet. Afrika had done enough ironing in her life when she'd been called up to the great house before holidays and parties to help. She knew the heft, the weight of the iron in her hand.

Lucy followed Afrika's gaze. Not one word needed to be spoken. Afrika merely inclined her head slightly toward the iron and trivet and then went over and picked them both up. She motioned again with her head toward the door.

There was something wonderful about this communication. They both walked ever so quietly to the door, Afrika gripping the iron. At Afrika's nod, Lucy flung the trivet into the middle of the floor. There was a scurrying of feet. The door opened.

In one swift gesture, Afrika stepped forward and swung the iron as hard as she could. *Crack*. Blood gushed from the woman's mouth, and then she fell unconscious to the floor. Lucy saw it all very clearly from where she stood. Two teeth had chittered across the wooden floor.

Suddenly Dulcey was there, screaming. Once more Afrika took the iron. Dulcey raised her hands, shouting, "No . . . no, don't!" She looked over at Lucy. "Miss Bradford, I promise I meant no harm." Lucy's face was grim with anger.

Afrika lowered the iron. "Get down on the floor now." Afrika turned to Lucy. "I know how to tie her real good. You come here and hold this iron over her head."

In a matter of seconds, Afrika had torn a table-cloth into strips and was binding and gagging Dulcey. "We better tie the other one, too," Afrika said. "She going to be waking up soon and be screaming out the rest of her teeth."

The tide was high, and *Winsome* rocked gently in her mooring slip. She was a welcome sight. Lucy had not been out sailing for several long weeks. She supposed the lovely sloop would be sold or put in storage now that her grandfather was dead.

"Quick, Afrika," Lucy said, springing aboard. "Take off those stern lines." She nodded toward the rear of the boat. It was only a matter of minutes before Lucy had yanked on the jib and raised it. Once out into the harbor she raised the main. Afrika proved herself amazingly adept about the myriads of ropes, winches, cleats, and running stays that combined to make a finely tuned little sailing vessel.

"You must have some experience," Lucy said after they had raised the main.

"Only been on a boat twice. Once, spent most my time hiding in a barrel full of crabs. The other time, comin' up here on the *Cameo,* I hid in the chain locker."

The wind was languid, and the sails flapped lazily in the night air. Lucy scanned the rigging where the telltales, small strings tied to the shrouds, would begin to flutter and indicate the wind direction at the first breeze. But they were becalmed. She had been staring so hard at the telltales for signs of wind that she did not hear the rhythmic dip of the oars of an approaching skiff.

"All right, girls. I have a Colt Walker trained on your head, Lucy Bradford. I can either blow your head off or sink your boat. You have no value to me alive. But your companion here is worth quite a bit." The drawl was still there, but that was all. Edmund de Rosey's voice was that of a cold, passionless killer.

Something within Lucy grew deathly still. Her heart did not race. It seemed to stop and drop right out of her.

"Do you hear me?" he barked.

Afrika bolted to the cockpit. Now she was trembling. Had she come this far only to end up back at Marlymont?

"You realize that you are in possession of stolen property. That the law of the land, the law of the Commonwealth of Massachusetts, gives me the right to reclaim this property in the name of its rightful owners."

How dare he! But she could not find her voice. Her heart, however, began beating furiously in her chest.

"This is an act of piracy, Lucy Bradford."

Something within Lucy clicked in response to that single word. A slight breeze ruffled the sail, and with it came another voice. *Yes, I break the law. I am an outlaw in my own dear Common-wealth. A pirate, I suppose, declaring his own law. . . .*

Well, if she were to be a pirate, she would be a crafty one. So she must not sound too bold. "Mr. de Rosey, you have a point. But you will have to come and collect your property, because she is damaged."

"How do you mean?"

"I believe she broke her ankle in the scuffle back on Fruit Street. She cannot walk. I nearly had to carry her all the way here. You are going to have to lift her over the rails, and seeing as I am under sail and you are not, you have the advantage of maneuverability."

It all sounded perfectly reasonable. She hoped the quaver in her voice appeared as fear and not as the nearly insane rage that was coursing through her bloodstream.

"All right," he said quickly. "I shall come up on your port side and tie on to the cleat. Remember, I shall be holding my revolver, cocked and ready."

"Yes, sir," she said meekly. And when she glanced at Afrika, the girl grabbed her ankle and held it as if in pain.

The breeze had picked up slightly from her port quarter, but Lucy did not let the sail fill. She had to maintain a low speed so de Rosey could come up to *Winsome*'s port side.

His face was pale in the moonlight and void of any expression as he rose up over the side. He had the revolver aimed at her chest. "All right, hands up. You don't need to steer now, just let the sails go, and get the girl up."

"I beg your pardon, sir. I can't help her if my hands are up."

He pressed his lips together and considered for a moment.

"All right, I'll help her." He glanced only briefly at Afrika, collapsed in the corner.

Lucy put her foot on the spoke of the wheel and stepped down. She crossed her legs and, as if shifting her weight, put another foot on the next spoke.

The deadly design began. The rudder turned; the wind stole up the other side of the sail just as Edmund stood on the deck. She didn't hear the muffled slap of the wind hitting the sail in a jibe, just the crack as the boom snapped across the cockpit and caught him square in the throat. He was hurled into the sea.

Lucy scrambled to the side and peered over the rail. He floated lifeless, his neck broken. Then he began to sink. Lucy quickly untied the skiff and went back to her helm.

"He's dead?"

"Yes," Lucy answered grimly. "See that rope by your feet, Afrika?"

"Yes, Miss Lucy."

"Don't call me Miss Lucy, just Lucy. Take that rope and shorten up on it. Then take the line on the starboard side. That's the side you're on. Pull it in tight and wrap it around that winch. We've got a good breeze, and with luck we can make Newburyport by dawn all downwind."

Lucy knew that she had become not just an outlaw but a murderer. There would be no turning back now. And the penalty for Afrika's role in it would probably be far worse. Newburyport was the logical destination. She remembered her grandfather talking about stations in Newburyport and agents. Somehow she and Afrika would find them.

The wind freshened, the stars broke through the clouds, and *Winsome* became a sprightly thing cutting through the white caps. The farther they got from land, out across the bay, the better Lucy felt. She would not permit herself to think about Edmund de Rosey. Surging seas pressed on the rudder, bringing the very pulse of the sloop into her hands.

Winsome sprinted across the billowing swells with the wind abaft the beam under the cold blaze of a million stars. Afrika, her head flung back, looked for the Drinking Gourd and found it straight over the top of the mast. She followed its handle to the tip where it pointed to the North Star. Taking a deep breath, she allowed herself to relax for a moment. *Steal away.* She was still on her way.

Lucy leaned her hip into the wheel. Her hair fell loose around her shoulders. The winged sprays of saltwater began to break from the bow. She might be a pirate, but her saltwater angel had returned. She headed True North.

The Bradford house remained in a tumult of grief for days on end. Lucy's disappearance sank them into agony, alternating with false hopes triggered by rumors of sightings. It never occurred to anyone in the family to check the Charles slip for *Winsome*. Then, nearly ten days after Lucy had disappeared, *Winsome* was found adrift four miles off Cape Ann, and a piece of trim from the dress that Lucy was last seen wearing was found in the cockpit. Her fate seemed to be sealed.

The house plunged into mourning. Sherbourne Bradford locked himself in his bedroom and saw no one. A thousand times a day he asked himself what in the name of God would have possessed his youngest daughter to go out sailing alone? Could she have been so grief-stricken over her grandfather's death that she would actually take her own life? It was unthinkable.

Two days after *Winsome* was found, Henry Van Schuyler appeared at the door of 136 Beacon Street and requested to speak alone with Sherbourne Bradford. He was insistent that Mr. Bradford see him. The girls remarked that Henry's entire manner had changed. It was more than the soberness of a person making a call on a house in grief. There was something else. The very light in his eye seemed different.

In the privacy of Sherbourne Bradford's study, Henry Van Schuyler reported that the body of Edmund de Rosey had been discovered by some fishermen. Badly decomposed, the body was identified only by a signet ring. It was worn by members of a secret society known as the Improved Order of the Red Men.

"Improved Order of the Red Men?" Sherbourne Bradford blinked. "What the devil is that?"

"A bizarre group of Southern gentlemen whose activities and practices are almost entirely shrouded in secrecy. More and more, however, we are finding that they are linked into a system of spies and false stations — through financing, mostly — dedicated to interrupting the work of the Underground Railroad and abolitionists."

"Well, if it is so secret, how do you know about it, Henry?" Sherbourne Bradford paused. "And of whom are you speaking when you say 'we'?"

Henry's face became grimmer. "It pains me to tell you that I have appeared in this house and enjoyed your kind hospitality, sir, under somewhat false pretenses."

"False pretenses?" Sherbourne whispered the words.

"It is true, of course, that I am a cousin of Elwyn. And it is true that I have been working at the Van Schuyler brokerage firm in New York. It is also true, as I am sure you have heard rumors, that I am not possessed of the financial acumen of Elwyn. Yet I am not quite as bad as I have led some to believe."

Sherbourne Bradford rose from his chair, troubled. "So what the devil are you?"

"I am, sir, a Pinkerton man."

"A Pinkerton man?"

"You have heard of the detective agency, sir?"

"Yes, yes, of course. But I thought they were out in Chicago."

"Yes, that is where Allan Pinkerton began the detective agency eight years ago, after he left the Chicago police force."

The fog began to clear from Sherbourne's eyes. He leaned forward now with great interest. "And I thought they mostly specialized in railway crimes, theft on the rails."

"That is all true. But Mr. Pinkerton has always been empathetic to the Northern and the abolitionist causes; he himself runs a station outside of Chicago. He is quite determined to track down every slave catcher in the country."

"And you are a Pinkerton detective?" A slow smile broke across Mr. Bradford's face.

"Yes, sir. It seems rather preposterous, doesn't it? The poor relative of the great and powerful New York Van Schuylers; the dim-witted, chubby cousin for whom they made a special position in the brokerage firm. It's a perfect cover."

"And Elwyn, does he know about this?"

"He will by tomorrow. I am resigning from the brokerage house. Allan Pinkerton has a very special assignment for me. But I must beg of you that you not reveal this to anyone at this time. I shall also ask Elwyn not to tell a soul. And . . ." For the first time in the interview, Henry Van Schuyler seemed unsure of himself.

"Yes?"

"I was about to say that I do wish that I could have told Lucy all along. She had such a profound contempt for me." He looked down, avoiding Sherbourne Bradford's eyes.

Daisy was told by her father to forget Edmund de Rosey completely. His real business was revealed, and this news alone was sufficiently disturbing to obliterate any feelings of regret or real grief about his death. "Unfortunate" was the most emotional word permitted. And Daisy, if she had had any notions of becoming the suffering victim of unrequited love or a love tragically cut off by death, was quickly disabused of these, first and foremost by her own mother.

"He was a spy, and he did it all for money," Emeralda said in a weary voice. "It had nothing to do with principles, his belief in our institutions of the South. He was no better than a horse thief. I shan't hear another word about him."

* * *

Although both Lucy and Edmund de Rosey had died in the cold waters of the Massachusetts Bay, no one ever connected the two events. Not even Henry Van Schuyler or his colleagues at the Pinkerton detective agency.

It had been decided that the wedding would not be postponed again. Instead it would be reduced even further. There would be no reception or ball at Brookdale. They would have a morning service at King's Chapel, with breakfast to follow at 136 Beacon. The flowers would all be white, a reminder of Lucy.

Iris wrinkled her nose at this. White flowers in November was not her idea of a celebration of marriage. But she dared not even suggest pale pink to her mother. The dresses, made in an array of rose colors, would remain, as the fabric had already been ordered. But Emeralda would not wear her signature emeralds.

So, in a sense, there was as much talk about the wedding as ever. A new challenge had been delivered: how to carry off such an event with taste and restraint but still show off the money and material wealth that was so important to Emeralda?

Toward the middle of August, Emeralda began to despair of Sherbourne being up to even the simplest of ceremonies. He refused to leave his room and insisted on being served all his meals there. He did not shun the society of his wife and remaining daughters, for he invited them to join him. But they were finding him depressing, for he often forgot to shave, and food stained his dressing gown.

Finally, toward the end of August, Sherbourne descended the staircase for the first time in weeks. He was shaved, and he sat at the dining room table for dinner. Except for his pallor, he appeared normal, but he was deathly silent. He moved through the days that followed like a hollow man. The conversation of the newly revised wedding plans swirled around him. He was acquiescent to everything his wife proposed, but he commented on nothing.

Chapter 32

October 25, 1858
New Hampshire

There was a raucous screech, and then the air was filled with the chittering sound of small birds. Lucy opened her eyes. She and Afrika had slept under a maple, and the last of its leaves flared in the early morning light. Overhead, storms of yellow finches flew here and there, now alighting on a tree, then swooping off in the morning air. The smell of dead, wet leaves permeated everything. But they were comfortable.

At the last station the deacon and his wife had given them a heavy blanket and an oilskin tarp. They were more than halfway up through New Hampshire. Between this point and the border, they had been told, the villages and the stations were few and far between. They would have to camp out.

Lucy was enjoying it, but Afrika was apprehensive for Lucy's sake. After they had landed in Newburyport, it had been Lucy's notion to set *Winsome* adrift. They had sailed as close as they could to the rocks and jumped out in waist-deep water. Their clothes had become drenched, and the weather turned unseasonably chilly. Lucy had caught a bad cold, which turned into pneumonia. By the time they left the Newburyport station and crossed over into New Hampshire, Lucy was delirious with fever.

Afrika nearly had to carry Lucy to the next station, which they had been told would have a row of white-painted bricks around its chimney. Afrika had then also become sick, and the two girls were too ill to continue. For two weeks, they stayed at a farmer's house near Manchester. Afrika begged Lucy to go back to her family in Boston. But Lucy would hear nothing of it.

She always answered the same. "I shall go back, but not now. Not until I see you across the border into Canada. I have missed Pap, and somehow this helps. Please, let me stay with you just to the border, and then I shall go back."

There was no need to ask. But for Afrika, who

had spent a lifetime aching for the mother she had lost, it was difficult to understand that someone would choose to stay away from her family.

Lucy sat up now. "Frost!" she whispered quietly. She had only been looking at the sky and the birds and had not noticed how everything sparkled under the silver coverlet of frost. Afrika still slept. Lucy thought she had never seen anything quite so beautiful. It was in that moment that Lucy knew that she herself had been transformed, strengthened.

Months ago she had gone owling with her grandfather, but it seemed like a lifetime ago. She remembered how much she had feared the night, but loved the deep silence. She remembered that she had wondered if she would ever grow accustomed to the night and find in the darkness a calm, a refuge, and even in the silence an unspoken meaning. She had now, and she knew that although she would never stop missing Pap and would soon begin to miss Afrika, she would never be lonely again.

On the night before they crossed the border into Canada, Afrika told Lucy the story of her baby.

"No, I got no more tears," Afrika repeated.

Afrika did not know her own age, but Lucy was sure that she and Afrika could not be more than a year apart. She knew Afrika's story was the truth. "He forced you," she said. "He forced you."

It had started to snow, and they had found shelter in the foundations of an old sugar house.

Afrika turned her back to Lucy and began to take off the heavy wrap, and then she unbuttoned her blouse. She removed it and the chemise so she was naked from the waist up. A blaze of cold moonlight illuminated the awful spiderweb that stretched across Afrika's back.

Crying softly, Lucy traced the terrible embroidery of scars with her finger. It was then that the unimaginable became imaginable.

That night, the two girls fell asleep in each other's arms. Afrika dreamed of Christmas, nearly a year before. The dream came clear, not jumbled like the others. It was as fresh as if it were just happening. And she could hear each voice and every word.

* * *

"Big Times is coming," said one of the little dusty-haired children.

"Massa says as long as that Yule log burns, that's how long the Big Times going to last. You excited 'bout Big Times, Frieda?" said another.

No, she wasn't, but she didn't want to tell the little ones why — that the holiday would give that dog more time to fool with her. Ramp saw how she looked lately. He'd come up that very day just a few minutes after she heard the children talking and said Big Times comin' and so's Moses.

"Moses? You mean that Moses?" Afrika asked.

"I do. You be ready. It be Sunday night in the Big Times. Everybody be in church. You hear the song, you know she's here."

And she heard the song. It came not on Sunday but a night earlier, just before midnight on Saturday.

"Steal away, steal away to Jesus. . . ."

How often had she heard that old hymn and hated it, but tonight there was one faint scratchy voice that drifted out from the pines. Then slowly other voices rose from the quarters in response.

"I ain't got long to stay here.
My Lord he calls to me.
He calls me by the thunder.
The trumpet sounds within my soul.
I ain't got long to stay here.
Steal away home."

Afrika gathered the few things she had into a bundle. She wrapped some ash cake and corn bread into a scarf. She left.

Now, with Lucy, she slept less than a mile from the Canadian border. She turned over and whispered, "We're gettin' out."

Chapter 33

November 1858

136 Beacon Street,
Boston, Massachusetts

Lucy slipped into the coal keep. She was sure that Harry had had the fires going for hours, and he would not need to get in for any more fuel. She knew she had to stay hidden.

It had wrenched her heart to see her father in the church. She had wanted to run to him. He looked like a shadow to her. A walking dead man. But she knew she must wait. She had no idea that the very day she returned to Boston would be the day of Iris's wedding. As she had recalled, they had not really settled on an exact date when she had left.

The irony was almost too much. Even in the coal keep she could hear the burble of gay voices, of celebration. She was terribly tired.

Thanks to the Fosters in Manchester, she had

been given enough money to take the train back. Still, she felt overwhelming fatigue and a certain disorientation. It had not been easy saying good-bye to Afrika. And now, for the first time, the emotion that had charged her for months seemed to drain out of her.

She leaned her head against a pile of kindling and began to doze off. She wasn't sure how long she had been asleep when she was awakened by the strong urge to go to the privy. She pressed her ear to the door and listened. There were no footsteps in the hall. She opened the door and stepped out.

This was the precise moment that Emeralda and Sherbourne Bradford came up from the cellar carrying a bottle of very fine champagne that had been chilling all morning in a bucket taken from the coal keep.

Emeralda's scream seemed to go on forever. Then the cork of the champagne blasted off. Her mother collapsed, unconscious, on the floor.

People came rushing in from the dining room. Sherbourne's eyes grew huge. Immense tears rolled down his face. "Lucy!" he cried. "Lucy!"

*   *   *

At the very moment that Lucy slipped into the coal keep at 136 Beacon, Afrika arrived in St. Catherine's, Canada, a town with a growing number of fugitive slaves. The next day she would begin school. It was not a pit school, but a school that stood proudly on one of the main streets of St. Catherine's. Light streamed through the windows and filled the school. Afrika learned quickly, and within one week she wrote her first letter to Lucy in Boston.

Chapter 34

December 31, 1862

Boston, Massachusetts

Lucy entered through the side door of the King's Chapel Church on Tremont. She had chosen to come in through the side because she did not want to see too many people at first. She needed to take her time and be alone with her thoughts.

She had many friends in attendance that night, and, of course, the entire Vigilance Committee was present. The next day, on the first of January of the new year 1863, Lincoln's Emancipation Proclamation would be in effect.

No one noticed the small figure in her cape and bonnet, slipping into a pew. She did not kneel in prayer, but after she had thanked God for this day, and for Mr. Lincoln, she thought of those who could not be there with her: Afrika, of course, who was well settled in Canada now; Pap, who would have held his head high once more as a citizen in his dearly beloved city.

At that moment, a large man made his way down the aisle. He scanned the audience and, when he finally spotted Lucy, turned into her pew. "Henry!" Lucy whispered and patted his hand. "I'm so glad you made it."

Henry Van Schuyler looked considerably older. Still plump, he had begun to go gray at the temples. The war had taken its toll. As the Pinkerton director in charge of gathering military intelligence for the Union forces, he lived under constant pressure. He looked weary tonight, but he would not have missed this event for anything. When he had heard of Lucy's return nearly four years earlier, he had come to Boston. She and her father and Elwyn were the only ones who knew of his work. Lucy and Henry had remained good friends ever since.

Now as the people in the church gathered, an unusual silence descended upon them. Then, at the stroke of midnight, bells all over Boston began to peal. The congregation in the church still remained silent. And in their silence, the people felt a bond with each other. For every person there — through money, or courage, or cunning — had defied the law of the land and helped a slave to freedom. Lucy's eyes filled as she rejoiced in the good will that surged around her.

❖

Henry Van Schuyler died of a heart attack shortly after the surrender at Appomattox.

Robert Shaw died leading Massachusetts' 54th Regiment in an assault on Fort Wagner in Charleston, South Carolina.

Lucy Bradford worked providing services to the needy of Boston over the next several years until her marriage to Franklin Wentworth, who supported his wife in all her endeavors. These included her insistence on keeping an independent bank account and setting up a trust for special causes. Both of these she managed herself with the advice of her husband and Elwyn Van Schuyler.

Three years after coming to St. Catherine's, Afrika married Buck Langdell, a fugitive slave ten years older who had escaped from a plantation in Maryland. Afrika became a schoolteacher in the same school where she had learned how to read and later became a teacher of teachers in a seminary near St. Catherine's. Both the seminary and the school where Afrika had learned to read were the recipients of donations from the Lucy Bradford Wentworth Foundation.

Lucy and Afrika, however, did not meet again for more than five decades.

Epilogue

November 2, 1917

154 Beacon Street,

Boston, Massachusetts

Afrika Langdell adjusted her hat and put on her spectacles to resume reading the letter as the taxi made its way from the station.

> . . . My sisters, except for Delphy, never forgave me. In their minds I had spoiled the wedding. Made what had been planned as an elegant affair into a shriveled-up cold-roast Puritan Boston ritual — just like my father's family. Iris had been cheated out of the kind of wedding she really deserved. At least that's the feeling I get now, and half a year has passed.
>
> How Lucy spoiled the wedding. It's becoming a legend, almost. But then again, people have a convenient way of molding realities to fit their own illusions. You see, up until that moment they thought I was dead, and not that they weren't re-

lieved to see me alive after all those months, but my timing in their eyes was regrettable. Don't tell me that my sisters, except for Delphy, weren't a teeny-tiny bit mad, even though I stood before them quite alive.

That letter, dated May 5, 1859, had been one of the early ones. From the middle of one century and into another, a course of more than fifty years, Afrika and Lucy had exchanged nearly one thousand letters. Over these years, there had been more weddings, none of which were spoiled by Lucy — except perhaps her own to Franklin Wentworth when she eloped. As she had said, though, everyone was so pleased to see the old maid finally married that it had barely made a difference that the two chose to run off. But now for the first time in nearly sixty years Afrika and Lucy would meet again in cold-roast Boston.

The taxi came and stopped in front of 154 Beacon Street. Afrika paused a moment and took a deep breath before stepping out onto the runningboard of the taxi. The driver held the door open.

Inside the house, a young girl of no more than ten pushed aside the heavy drapery. Outside, the day was misty. She could just make out the taxi. Then she saw the figure.

"Grandma! She's here!" she whooped. "She's coming up the stairs, Grandma, and she doesn't have a cane."

"Well, then, I'm not going to use mine."

Slowly Lucy Bradford Wentworth made her way across the entry hall. Her hand, gnarled and swollen with arthritis, grasped the brass knob. She opened the heavy door and moved out onto the top of the stoop. She peered through the fog of her own old eyes into the swirling mists outside. A small, erect figure, trim with a hat and veil, stood perfectly still on the third step.

"Lucy!"

"Afrika!"

Time stopped. The two old women stood for a full minute. Then Lucy extended both her hands. "Welcome to my grandfather's house."

About This Book

When I was a child growing up in the Midwest in the 1950s, much of the American history we were taught was sanitized or made pleasantly palatable for impressionable young minds. I acquired, needless to say, very peculiar and inaccurate ideas concerning certain key events in our country's history, especially those surrounding the Civil War and slavery. Most of my ideas about slavery came from Hollywood, just as most of my notions about the Native Americans and the western frontier also came from Hollywood. There was a technicolor brilliance to everything, and all the men in the Westerns looked like Roy Rogers or John Wayne, and all the women looked like Dale Evans.

As young history students, we knew that slavery was wrong, and we also knew that coming from Indiana we were on the right side, the winning side in the Civil War. But that was about all we knew. We had, in effect, learned some of the facts, but not the deeper truths. And it is one thing to know that slavery is wrong, but quite another to learn of the vilest aspects of its tyranny. We had, for example, heard very few stories of how slave families actually had been torn apart, mothers whose children were sold, or the terrible sexual exploitation of young black girls and women. The teachers and the curriculum they taught intended to protect us from that just as they protected us in our Indiana history course from the fact that my home state had been the place of the rebirth of the Ku Klux Klan in the twentieth century.

We must have, at some point, been told something about the Underground Railroad, but in such a way that it had acquired a rather quaint charm. Half-myth, half-history, the Underground Railroad shaped up in my immature, untutored mind as something like a ride at Disneyland. And most amazing of all, I don't recall hearing the name Harriet Tubman. Such was the condition of my hometown's history curriculum some thirty-five years ago.

It was through my own children's very excellent history curriculum in the public schools of Cambridge, Massachusetts, that I first began to realize just how much I had missed. So I began reading.

Boston has always been considered a bastion of liberal thinking, a spawning ground for such great abolitionists and defenders of liberty as Wendell Phillips and William Lloyd Garrison. But through extensive research I came to realize that slavery could not have even made it out of the seventeenth century and into the eighteenth century if it had not been for the support of such cities in the North like Boston. The truth is this: Many of those families whose names have become inextricably intertwined with Harvard and the China Trade and the great New England fortunes are the very same families whose economic empires were totally dependent upon a slave-based economy.

A writer of historical fiction is often asked: What really happened in your story? What is true, and what did you make up? From my perspective, everything I have written about in *True North* really happened in one way or another. That is not to say that I did not take liberties in manipulating some events. But I would call them liberties as opposed to licenses, for I have always tried to write within the structures of logic and judicious imagination and to never disturb what I perceive to be the tenor of the times or the essential fabric of the society.

For example, when I was reading former slave William Still's exhaustive account of the Railroad's passengers and their history, I could not help but be impressed by the ingenious ways in which station agents concealed the fugitives. I did not read that anyone had ever been concealed in a clock, but there were equally novel solutions. And in fact, one fugitive slave, a man named Henry Brown, climbed into a box that a carpenter nailed shut and had himself shipped to the North!

Between the years 1852 and 1857, Harriet Tubman usually made two trips south a year to lead people out of slavery to the North. Most of her documented trips were within the region of Maryland and Dorchester County. However, wanted posters and handbills about her were posted far beyond that region. There is no documentation that she ever went as far as Virginia and the region of the Great Dismal Swamp, but not every trip she made was known, and it is not unrealistic to think she might have entered that area. In December of 1860, Miss Tubman brought out her last party of fugitive slaves and saw them safely to Philadelphia.

Although the Bradford family was a real historical family, and indeed William Bradford, the colonial leader, traveled on the *Mayflower* and was a signer of the original Mayflower Compact as well as the first governor of the Plymouth Plantation, Lucy Bradford and her sisters and parents and grandfather are fictional "descendents" that I have created for the purposes of this book. Afrika, too, is a fictional creation, but one based on the sad histories I read of many young slave girls. Many other characters such as Austin Bearse, Robert Gould Shaw, Wendell Phillips, Francis Parkman, Charles Francis, and Abigail Adams were real people who lived in Boston at that time. And although Henry Van Schuyler was not real, the Allen Pinkerton detective agency for which he worked was very real and very much involved in espionage activities for the Union during the Civil War. My information concerning the Boston Vigilance Committee and details of how and where they met and the stations that were used was largely derived from Austin Bearse's *Reminiscences of Fugitive-Slave Law Days in Boston.*

Thomas Garrett and Eliza and Ezekiel and John Hunn were all real stationmasters on the Underground Railroad. It is also true that the Alcott family in Concord and Ralph Waldo Emerson served as stationmasters.

Finally, one must bear in mind that among these real people, those who were members of the Boston Vigilance Committee constituted a minority within a city which prided itself as being a cradle of democracy and a noble defender of individual liberty and freedom.

—Kathryn Lasky
September 1995
Cambridge, Massachusetts

For Further Reading:

Bearse, Austin. *Reminiscences of Fugitive-Slave Law Days in Boston.* Printed by Warren Richardson, Boston: 1880.

Blockson, Charles L. *Hippocrene Guide to the Underground Railroad.* Hippocrene Books, New York: 1994.

Cosner, Sharon. *The Underground Railroad.* Franklin Watts, New York: 1991.

Hamilton, Virginia. *Anthony Burns: The Defeat and Triumph of a Fugitive Slave.* Knopf, New York: 1988.

Haskins, Jim. *Get on Board: The Story of the Underground Railroad.* Scholastic, New York: 1993.

Lester, Julius. *To Be a Slave.* Dial Books, New York: 1968.

Mellon, James, ed. *Bullwhip Days: The Slaves Remember, an Oral History.* Weidenfeld & Nicholson, New York: 1988.

Petry, Ann. *Harriet Tubman: Conductor on the Underground Railroad.* Simon & Schuster, New York: 1996.

Siebert, Wilbur. *The Underground Railroad from*

Slavery to Freedom. Russel & Russel, New York: 1967.

Sterling, Dorothy. *The Story of Harriet Tubman.* Scholastic, New York: 1954.

Still, William. *The Underground Railroad.* Ebony Classic, Johnson Publishing Company, Chicago: 1970.

ABOUT THE AUTHOR

Kathryn Lasky is the author of many books, both fiction and nonfiction, including *Sugaring Time*, for which she won a Newbery Honor. Among her fiction books are *The Night Journey*, a winner of the National Jewish Book Award; and *Beyond the Burning Time*, an ALA Best Book for Young Adults. She has also received the *Boston Globe-Horn Book* Award as well as *The Washington Post* Children's Book Guild Award for her contribution to nonfiction.

Ms. Lasky and her husband live in Cambridge, Massachusetts.